Sherlock Holmes and Hitler's Messenger of Death

Petr Macek

First edition published in 2017

Paperback ISBN 978-1-78705-049-5
ePub ISBN 978-1-78705-050-1
PDF ISBN 978-1-78705-051-8

Published in the UK by MX Publishing
335 Princess Park Manor, Royal Drive,
London, N11 3GX

www.mxpublishing.com

Cover design by Brian Belanger

FOREWORD

As I sit down at my writing desk the blood on my clothes and hands has still not dried. My hair reeks of smoke and I can barely recognise my own face in the mirror. But the thought of washing up and changing my clothes, wiping away the horror of the past few hours, is unimaginable. What water can cleanse one's memory? What soap can rid the mind of the images it has seen? Can a clean pressed shirt absorb horror like gauze absorbs blood?

As a young doctor serving in Afghanistan during the war, I had seen my fair share of blood. Sometimes I had literally waded in it. Now, to retain my sanity, I had to write out my feelings, or at least try; to pour out everything that had happened to me and my friend in words, phrases, sentences. Perhaps that familiar acquaintance, the orderly world of ink strokes, lines and dots driven by the laws of grammar, would supply the necessary rationality.

I lied.

This is a confession that I have to make at the outset. I have lied to you, dear reader, so many times that I am unable to count the lies. It began with my withholding certain circumstances, which – to remain hidden – led to more and more untruths. Is the fact that I was compelled to do it any excuse? I do not know and I shall leave it to your discretion. I add only that I have always acted in the greater interest of my country, for the safety of my family and my friend, and for peace of mind. And if I have misappropriated this forced bending of reality, and set aside the most sensitive aspects of the matter, I always, after careful consideration, chose to destroy the manuscript. Or at least seal and bury it until my memories could no longer do harm.

I can, however, assure those who devour my texts in wonder at the detective's abilities that in this respect I have never fabricated or embellished. I self-censored only where sensitive political and social matters called for it, never for, let us say, professional reasons.

The truth is that for all the adventures of the great detective I have published, there are still more that have been left unwritten. I would like to see a library shelf a hundred or a hundred and fifty years from now. How many cases of Sherlock Holmes will bear the name of my publisher, Mr Doyle, and how many will bear the names of others? And the lines that I write now I write knowing that no one will read them in a long time. But they are important to me, so I will treat them with the same care as all texts that I submit for publication.

In order to continue, therefore, I must first correct certain claims made in previous books, mainly *His Last Bow: Some Reminiscences of Sherlock Holmes* and *From the Files of Sherlock Holmes*. My friend's last case was not the capture of the German spy Von Bork on the eve of the Great War. His actions led further, much further.

The war is now long over. As far as I know, another will soon be upon us. When I look behind me, on the floor near the door of the hotel, I see a rolled up newspaper. The errand boy squeezed it through the letterbox a few moments ago. I had asked him for it. It is night, the other guests had long since dismembered all available copies, but apparently someone from the staff collected them. The date printed on the header is May 6, 1937. This is an evening edition, but of course it does not contain the events that had just occurred a short while before.

I tremble, but not from cold or age.

How I wish I could write a different date for Holmes's last case! The fact is that I do not know it myself. Perhaps, if he survives tonight, he will still be able to solve another.

If he survives…

I

God Save the Queen

We had first laid eyes on that face more than forty years ago.

The face was written in the history of the British Empire in black letters. But the first time we saw it was not in the courtroom or in prison or in the criminal files of Scotland Yard, or even out in the field during our investigations. No, the first place we saw it was in the reception salon of our dear Queen Victoria. And right away I must correct myself: the phrase "written in history" does not entirely apply in his case. His acts were so hideous that his existence will certainly be stricken from the records to the last letter.

But let us not get ahead of ourselves.

The event to which I must at the start of my story return dates to the spring of 1894. To my and everyone's surprise, Holmes had returned, after many years of being presumed dead, to the world of the living. Perhaps it is needless to describe here the well-known circumstances that led him to falsify his own death. I only point out that it was at a time when the members of the late Professor Moriarty's criminal network, whom Holmes had succeeded in dispersing, were seeking revenge.

The detective's resurrection also piqued the interest of the otherwise phlegmatic Queen, who, despite avoiding public life, invited him several weeks after his return for a private audience, to which I had the honour of accompanying him.

The meeting with the great monarch took place over a cup of tea at five o'clock in Buckingham Palace. This in itself suggested her extraordinary curiosity. It was no secret that the Queen had little affection for London. Ever since the death of her husband, Prince Albert, she had spent most of her time at Windsor Castle or Balmoral. Thus it had been for the last thirty years. Her appearances at Buckingham Palace were rare indeed, and the fact that she had chosen it as the setting for her meeting with Holmes was in and of itself something of an event.

The Queen received us in a decorated music salon on the first floor of the palace. Also present at the audience were Frederick Fawcett, the young secretary of the outgoing Prime Minister William Gladstone, Undersecretary of State for Home Affairs George W. Russell, the Queen's personal secretary Sir Henry Ponsonby and her Indian aide, Abdul Karim, who had taken the place of the deceased John Brown. Four Indian domestics under his command served the company.

The one new face for us was Fawcett, who had just recently taken up his new post. I reckoned he was about thirty. He was dressed in the latest fashion and possessed a fit, athletic figure, but his most pronounced feature was his expressive blue eyes. Russell we had already met during Holmes's engagement in *The Case of the Dancing Plague**, though he had held a different post at the time. The Queen's other closest advisors, Ponsonby and Karim, were not strangers to us either.

Munshi, as the Queen called Karim with his exotic appearance and aura, seemed engaged in a battle with Fawcett for the monarch's attention. The Indian enjoyed great influence with the Queen** and spoke with her in a mix of English and his native tongue. His gold and white turban decorated with a red silk sari with white bands contrasted sharply with the simple frilly black dress that the plump ruler wore.

The Queen was sitting majestically opposite Holmes, silently sipping tea with milk, while examining the detective's face and listening to his story.

"Astonishing, most astonishing," she said when he had finished telling her of the downfall of the diabolical Colonel Moran, Moriarty's right-hand man***. "To live in the shadows for almost three years; indeed, to sacrifice one's own life!"

"In my opinion your approach was needlessly theatrical," said Fawcett. "Had you cooperated with the authorities you would not have been compelled to hide at all."

The Queen raised her eyebrows and looked askance at the young man. She was not accustomed to anyone contradicting her opinion, moreover someone so young, whom she did not even know. She frowned indignantly and pursed her lips.

"If I am not mistaken, were it not for Mr Holmes the police would have been utterly unaware of Mr Moriarty's actions," she rebuked, setting aside the empty china cup.

Fawcett blinked, but dared not argue. He sullenly bit his teacake and pretended he had said nothing. Karim, standing just to the side of the Queen, waved to the servant to refill our cups.

"I did only what was logical given the circumstances," Holmes replied humbly, tactfully skipping the remark about the police. "I had to be invisible to inflict the deadly blow. I also dedicated some time to travel, which I consider to be of some benefit."

The Queen smiled at him kindly.

"You have shown us that law and order are not mere words," she said. "You did not bend to the villainous Moriarty, but risked your life defending the values on which this country has been built. Nor must we forget your heroism at Khartoum****, which my foreign minister has described to me. Sherlock Holmes, we are forever in your debt."

I blushed on behalf of the detective while he politely nodded. The septuagenarian ruler adjusted the Indian shawl draped over her shoulders and stood up with difficulty.

"Your service to the crown must be rewarded," she continued. "The deputy Prime Minister is present at the meeting because the Queen alone cannot grant you a decoration or order; the request must come from the office of the Prime Minister. Hereby the Queen would like, Mr Holmes, to express her thanks and appreciation. And I hope that the request, as far as the decoration is considered, will be conveyed to the office of the honourable Mr Gladstone," she added with a meaningful look at Fawcett.

He did not protest.

But Holmes suddenly stood up and pointed an accusatory finger at the Queen.

"No!" he exclaimed in alarm.

"Excuse me?" the Queen intoned. "Do you refuse my homage?"

"Karim, stop him at once!" Holmes cried, ignoring the Queen and leaping from his chair.

I was probably the first to realise that his warning was not directed at Her Majesty, but at one of the Indian servants, who had just poured more tea.

Neither Karim nor the others understood. They were paralysed with confusion. The detective gave the table a swift kick, sending the cup of tea and jug of milk tumbling to the floor, and despite strict protocol against touching the Queen, gently but firmly pushed her away from the maid. The stout ruler slipped back on the cushioned stool. Her crown slipped to one side, momentarily revealing the widow's cap on her head.

Ponsonby gasped and Karim glared at Holmes angrily. When I saw that he wanted to intervene, I could not hold back.

"The maid!" I shouted. "Holmes is protecting the Queen! There's poison in the cup!"

The dark eyes of the Indian girl, whose face was veiled from the nose down, sparkled maliciously. She bounded out of our reach and hurled the pot of tea at me. The water scalded my nose and cheek, indeed the whole right side of my face. I yelped in pain and tried to quickly dry the water

"Naya?!" Karim cried.

But he stood protectively between her and the Queen.

From the folds of her sari the maid took out a long, curved dagger and crouched in a fighting stance.

Everything happened in a few seconds.

The momentary shock of everyone in the room vanished in an instant. Before I could wipe my face a series of events took place with lightning speed. Russell ran from the salon into the hallway where I heard him call for the guards. While Karim shielded the Queen with his body, Ponsonby, no doubt remembering his instincts as a colonel in the Crimean War, gently picked up the ruler and carried her to safety. Fawcett led the three other Indians, trembling with fear and astonishment, to the side of the salon. And Holmes joined Karim, who together carefully closed in on the attacker, Naya.

The Indian woman snarled with fury as she was driven into a corner. The salon was rectangular except for a large semi-circular bay window. Now Naya faced down the two men and looked around frantically, searching for a way out.

Karim, who was responsible for the Indian servants, spoke to her in Hindu. I did not understand her reply, but clearly she was spitting insults at him.

Karim frowned and clenched his fists until his knuckles turned white.

"How did you discover her intentions, Holmes?" he asked, while they pushed Naya further back.

"Elementary. As she walked past me, I detected a weak odour of almonds."

"The tea biscuits? There was something in them?"

"Not at all. Those were already on the table. And the type of teacake that you serve does not contain bitter almonds. The scent that I detected came from the pot and is indicative of a high concentration of potassium cyanide."

Karim barked an insult at the would-be assassin in their native tongue.

"Gentlemen, you can discuss it later," Fawcett cried uneasily.

His captives were in a corner whispering excitedly among themselves.

"Catch her!"

From the neighbouring white drawing room and the Queen's chambers adjacent to the music salon, to which a moment ago Ponsonby had disappeared with the ruler, we heard the noise and clatter of running guards, as well as from the grand staircase in the hallway, where Russell had run for help.

Naya no longer waited.

While Karim lunged at the girl's arm with a dagger, the detective leapt at her and tried to take out her legs. At least that was his intention, although the girl did not cooperate. With agility I have never seen even in the circus, she jumped on the wall, from which she bounced into the air. She used the bent down Karim as a next step, and performed a graceful somersault right over his head and indeed about half of the room. Under other circumstances I would have applauded the acrobatic feat.

The only possible escape route remained the passage door into the blue parlour and from there across the state dining room to the gallery and ballroom.

Holmes and Karim immediately bounded after her.

"Watch them! God knows they may be her accomplices!" Fawcett cried to me and ran after them.

One look at the terrified servants, however, told me that they had nothing to do with the plot and were as horrified as we were. And the guards would be here any second; so I ignored his instruction and joined the chase.

The linear layout of the palace chambers simplified the chase, as did the trail of startled voices of servants as she sped through each room. As we chased after Naya from one room to the next, rooms that I would have never otherwise had the opportunity to see, I barely had time to admire the tapestries, crystal chandeliers, marble fireplaces, royal portraits and paintings by Rembrandt and Van Dyck. It was all just a blur.

But as I was in no way the athlete that Holmes or Fawcett were, it wasn't long before I was huffing and puffing, and it was all I could do just to keep up with them.

Between the gallery and the ballroom that extended behind it, the fleeing assassin crashed into the majordomo, who was walking obliviously in the opposite direction.

"Boothsby, look out!" Karim cried to the distinguished old gentleman, but to no effect.

Naya correctly concluded that one slender woman, even one clearly trained in the exotic martial arts, would not escape from four men and with the palace guard right behind them.

She therefore opted for a different tactic.

She leapt behind Boothsby and placed a dagger on his neck. Startled he dropped the mahogany sideboard he was carrying. Silverware clattered and flew across the floor.

We stopped on our heels and for a moment it was quiet while each side considered what to do next.

"Back!" the Indian woman ordered, and to demonstrate her resolve, cut the majordomo on the cheek.

Blood trickled down the old man's parchment-white skin into his whiskers and collar livery. He hissed and swatted at her, pulling the scarf from her mouth.

"But that isn't Naya!" Karim cried in astonishment.

"Who are you?" Holmes asked her.

She did not answer. She looked from one to the other of us and slowly backed away.

Holmes and I had already found ourselves in similar situations before, so I knew what my friend was thinking. He needed a weapon with which to confront the gleaming dagger. Naturally we had not brought one for our audience with the Queen; nor did the walls of the gallery present us with any decorative arms that he could use, and the guards had still not arrived.

His eyes fell on the fallen silverware.

Apparently Fawcett had the same idea. But instead of the silverware, he grasped a heavy, blue and gold vase, grabbing its leg like a club.

"The Sèvres porcelain of His Majesty George IV!" the majordomo piped in the muffled tone of a man responsible for the wares whose nearing retirement was now in jeopardy.

Karim followed Fawcett's example and removed a Chinese porcelain pagoda from the Oriental cabinet, heaving it like a grenade.

"A gift from the Abyssinian Emperor!" the hostage cried an octave higher.

The assassin realised that the hostage would not help her and pushed him with all her might against our group. As the squealing old man fell to the floor, she quickly bent down, grabbed the sharpest knife and hurled it at us.

The knife hurtled through the air, changed trajectory and landed with a heavy thud in the canvas of one of the paintings just behind us. We all looked at Boothsby, but instead of offering an interpretation of the Old Master in question, his eyes rolled up and he fainted dead away.

The woman took advantage of the confusion and before we could reach the unconscious butler, slammed behind her the lacquered French doors which connected the gallery to the ballroom and barricaded them with something. We crashed against it, but lost precious seconds. When we finally broke through it turned out that she had stuck a soup ladle through the handles.

The ballroom was empty.

The largest room in Buckingham Palace was breath-taking. A coffered ceiling, everywhere solid gold, the walls lined with red plush seats; but there was no sign of the assassin. Finally, the guards joined us and Karim quickly acquainted them with the situation. Several exits led from the hall, mostly to rooms for the servants. We agreed to split up. The palace guard would search the state chambers and corridors, while Fawcett and Karim searched one part of the service wing and Holmes and I the other.

We were now in a considerably less opulent part of the palace. Adjacent areas and service corridors used to serve guests of balls and receptions. A freight elevator led here carrying food from the kitchen; there was a series of tables, counters, sinks and furniture with serving equipment. In another room, we found some extinct fireplaces. Everywhere it was dark and cold. Outside too it was dark. At that time of year sundown was still early in the afternoon, and there was not a soul anywhere. Clearly the Queen did not use the palace very much.

"There are so many corners and shadows here that she could be hiding anywhere," I said, looking around nervously.

The uncomfortable feeling of being in a confined space was intensified by the memory of the Indian woman's sharp dagger. I would hate to discover her only to find the blade sticking in my back

"Quiet," said the detective, looking into the fireplace chimney. He listened to hear if she had not escaped this way. At least he was armed with a serving fork with two sharp prongs; but in the excitement in the gallery I had forgotten to equip myself.

I walked over to one of the service trolleys and leaned on it. Suddenly I felt a sticky fluid between my fingers.

Blood did not make me squeamish, although I did not know where it was coming from. But thanks to my years spent in the company of Holmes, I had a feeling it wasn't the dinner sirloin. I called to him and together we opened the service trolley.

A tiny body wrapped in a bloodstained sari rolled out onto the tiled floor. A shock of black hair peaked out from one side.

"The real Naya, I presume," said Holmes.

Suddenly, in the reflection of the shiny coins sewn on the edges of the dead woman's dress, a shadow moved. The detective abruptly pushed me aside before I had time to realise what was happening and rolled over on his other side.

Lodged in the spot where a moment ago we had been leaning over the dead body of the servant was an enormous meat cleaver.

One of us would have surely got it in the back of the head.

The assassin jumped out from the shadows and kicked me in the jaw with her bare foot. I fell back hard against the table, gasping for breath.

Holmes grasped the fork and lunged at her, but she fended off his attack with her dagger. They engaged in a bizarre battle: the tiny woman and the sinewy detective with weapons that no fencing school had ever seen. Sparks flew from the tips of the detective's fork and the girl's dagger. Time and again they lunged at each other, with neither gaining an advantage. But the assassin was incredibly agile, as we had already seen. She leapt onto the counter, aiming her weapon at Holmes's head, while she hopped from desk to desk like a monkey

I scrambled to my knees and looked for something I could use to help my friend. On the floor I felt the cleaver.

Then the clanging noise of the weapons attracted the attention of Karim and Fawcett, who had been searching a couple of rooms below. As soon as they saw the girl on the table with the dagger in her hand, Holmes facing her with the fork, and me on the floor in a pool of blood, they knew what to do. Fawcett ran towards me, probably thinking that I was injured, but after a few steps, slipped on a puddle of blood. As he swung his arms to maintain his balance or catch something, he pulled along poor Holmes, who was standing nearby, bringing him tumbling to the ground with him. The attacker, who at that moment nobody could stop, skipped over the table tops to the closed window and crashed through it. Neither the old wooden frame nor the glass could stop the live projectile and shards flew everywhere.

We helped each other to our feet and rushed to the window.

The remains of the window lay down below. But not the Indian girl.

"We are on the second floor," I said. "She must have been injured in the fall! She cannot be far. Send the guards outside!"

Karim pursed his lips and Fawcett wiped his sweaty brow.

"Had I not slipped so stupidly we could have gotten her," he said apologetically. "But where she has gone is a mystery."

This part of the palace was adjacent to a public street, now with only a few pedestrians and light traffic. Nobody was in a hurry; no one seemed alarmed by the assassin.

Holmes studied the vicinity. Despite the darkness, dotted here and there with little islands of light from the gas lanterns, he saw something.

"Look!" he cried, pointing.

A covered carriage was quickly receding in the distance where he pointed. It was so far away that we could not even hear the clatter of hooves. We could just make out a slender shadow slide from the roof like a cat and into the compartment.

The palace now felt even colder than it had before. Our audience with the Queen was over.

The subsequent investigation revealed that the carriage had been waiting for the assassin beneath the window. Karim was not blamed, because the attacker had only pretended to be Naya in order to gain access to the palace. Likewise, the majordomo Boothsby was not required to pay for the palace treasures destroyed in the chase.

Holmes and I never learned the assassin's motive. I do not know whether Her Majesty's investigators unravelled the case. The detective was not asked to take part in the investigation. Indeed, we were told in no uncertain terms not to discuss the incident with anyone. It and all circumstances around it were declared a state secret.*****

Not even in my wildest dreams would it have ever occurred to me that we had just met with an evil whose power and intensity had only just emerged.

* Apparently an as yet undiscovered case.

** Mohammed Abdul Karim (1863 – 1909) was Queen Victoria's Indian secretary and confidant during the last fifteen years of her reign. He won her trust and she apparently showed him maternal care. He liked using his influence over others and took advantage of the Queen's patronage for his personal gain.

*** The destruction of Colonel Sebastian Moran is recounted in *The Adventure of the Empty House* in the collection *The Return of Sherlock Holmes*.

**** During his hiatus Holmes travelled throughout Tibet, visited Lhasa and spent several days with the Dalai Lama, posing as a Norwegian traveller named Sigerson. He travelled through Persia, visited Mecca and stayed briefly in Khartoum, although exactly what he did there is unknown.

***** Queen Victoria's life was in danger on several occasions. The first was in 1840, when she was pregnant. Eighteen-year-old Edward Oxford fired at her with a pistol as she rode in a carriage. Oxford fired twice, but missed. He was convicted of treason, but the charges were lifted for reason of insanity. Further assassination attempts took place in 1842. John Francis fired at Victoria as she passed through St. James's Park, but he was promptly neutralised by a police officer. He was sentenced to death, but the sentence was later commuted to life imprisonment. John William Bean tried to shoot Victoria, though his pistol was loaded with paper balls and tobacco. His offence was nevertheless punishable by death. Prince Albert encouraged Parliament to pass a law according to which the use of weapons in the presence of the ruler in order to startle them could be punished by up to seven years in prison. Bean was thus sentenced to 18 months in prison. In 1887, Irish anarchists plotted to blow up Westminster Abbey during a service at which Victoria was to be present, but the plot was exposed.

II

The Trouble with Richard Green

So much time had passed since the failed attempt to assassinate Queen Victoria that I barely thought about it anymore. She died in January 1901 of entirely natural causes, leaving us the legacy of an empire that during her reign attained the summit of its political, industrial, scientific and military might. After her death it would never reach such heights again.

Naya and our other enemies, cases and adventures of those years gradually merged together in my mind. What I could I recorded in my journal and published periodically. My and Holmes's paths crossed and diverged. Life had chewed us up and spit us out, though each in a different way. In my old age I was alone*. Holmes never married, and in the end even resigned from detective work**, retiring to the countryside. When I finally bid adieu to my medical practice I moved in with him.

Old age has been merciful to us. At the start of 1937, which is when our story begins, we were both well over eighty, but still enjoyed alertness and good health. Whenever I wondered at it, my friend brushed it aside. He jokingly attributed it to the effects of the mysterious potion we had encountered in the cave laboratory of Dr Fu Manchu***. As scientists we could not accept the existence of an elixir of youth, but nevertheless our bodies enjoyed vitality, and living in the country made us even more robust.

On the other hand, many of our loved ones already had been called to the Kingdom of Heaven. We could no longer enjoy the comforts of our dear landlady Mrs Hudson, the dedicated global vision of Holmes's brother Mycroft, or the collegial taunting of Scotland Yard's Detective Lestrade. But others entered our lives.

Holmes took a particular interest in a certain Richard Green, a young man from a nearby farm. His keen mind and natural interest in nature and the world around him had impressed Holmes years ago, when the boy was still a child. Over time he came to Cuckmere Haven increasingly often and helped the retired detective with his bee colonies. As he grew, he began to share with him his interest in science, especially chemistry, which Holmes, sensing the development of the boy's innate talent, encouraged even more.

Had my friend had a son, I would have imagined him like this.

Then there was our new housekeeper, who took over the running of the household after the death of Mrs Hudson. She and her husband, Major Steiner, whom Holmes hired as a manager, gardener and occasional driver, moved in together. The Steiners came from Germany and had moved only recently to the English countryside. Steiner was a former soldier who had fought for Germany in the Great War, but apparently did not agree with the project his homeland was currently embarking on. But whether he had left Berlin voluntarily or under duress we did not know. His past was not discussed.

The backdrop of our quiet, sedentary life was the nearby town of Fulworth, where we frequently took afternoon strolls. We found kindred spirits in Pastor Whittaker, who had replaced the fraud Barlow****, and the local doctor, Dr Jack Conway, whom we would meet every Thursday for a game of whist. We would begin at four o'clock and remain at the table until late at night, when Major Steiner would pick us up in his car. I should point out that while Holmes' brilliant mind was without equal in matters of crime, in cards he was woefully inept. At the initial draw I always prayed that he would be paired with someone else.

My mind was thus pleasantly occupied during our afternoon stroll on the day when our adventure began. I was so engrossed in my thoughts that I only half listened to Holmes's droning monologue about the migration of bee colonies and was rather wondering what strategy to choose for the afternoon game. Paradoxically I was snapped back to attention by the detective's sudden silence. We were walking through the village to Dr Conway's office and had just found ourselves in front of the police station. The faces in the crowd of people hurrying by us were just a blur, but Holmes took particular note of one face.

"Strange, wouldn't you say my dear Watson?" he said. "Is that not Richard walking over there?"

Indeed, Holmes's protégé was crossing the street. He had not seen us yet, but stopped. He was apparently going to the police station, but a few steps from the door he seemed to changed his mind. He hesitated for a moment, and then abruptly turned around and sat on a bench, where he lit a cigarette. But it was not his nervousness and indecision that caught Holmes's attention, but the young man's very presence in the village. At the time, Richard was studying at the University of London, where he had been granted a scholarship, and only appeared in Fulworth on holidays and vacations.

That day was neither.

"I may not be young anymore, but I still remember my student years," said Holmes, stepping behind young Green and placing his hand on his shoulder. "In my day, the demands of lectures, consultations and exams during the semester were such that I did not have time to leave school. I would squat in my little room at Cambridge for days in order to master the problem. I am glad that today's students are so brilliant that they have time for everything. Welcome home, Richard."

The young man looked up, startled. The carefree and loving young man I knew was practically unrecognisable. Seeing a kindly smile in Holmes's usually austere face he relaxed and lowered his eyes. We exchanged greetings and, without invitation, sat beside him on the bench.

"I wanted to stop by tomorrow and say hello," he said with a sigh. "I thought I might help feed the bees. I needed to get out of town, clean up my head."

"Is everything all right?"

Richard drew on his cigarette and blew a cloud of smoke.

"Professor Biggles has greater demands on my knowledge of Greek philosophy than I am able to devote to its acquisition," he said slowly, shrugging his shoulders. "But in chemistry I am second to none."

"I have no doubt of it, young man. If your judgement is still as good as when I met you, I have no concern about your marks."

The dejected young man frowned, but apparently only I noticed it. Holmes was busy stuffing his pipe. While he was doing so, I inquired after the health of Green's parents, who lived in a farmhouse just outside the village, and asked him to convey my greetings. It seemed to me that he was glad when the subject turned from his studies; one did not have to be a brilliant detective like Holmes to see that.

I wondered why.

But we were not so close as for me to inquire about the reasons, and my friend, whom the young man may have responded to, did not evince any reaction. I thought perhaps that Richard's marks were not good enough and that he did not want to disappoint Holmes, who had encouraged him in his studies and even recommended him to the university.

The detective finally drew on his pipe and the air wafted with the aroma of tobacco.

"I presume you need a break from something other than school", he said, letting out a cloud of smoke.

Richard looked even more crestfallen and put his head in his hands.

"Perhaps a love affair?" I could not help asking.

"Gentlemen, with all due respect, there are things that really are none of your concern."

"Pardon me?" I said.

Holmes and I had not deserved that. But the remark seemed to hit the young man hard.

"Please leave me be," he sobbed. "My head is buzzing like a beehive, but this is something that your bee smoker****** cannot calm. If only I could..."

He turned his head away so we could not meet his eyes.

"I must face my problems alone," he added quietly.

"Very well then," said Holmes reluctantly.

He understood that further questioning would simply upset the boy even more.

"But if you are beset by something that I could help you with, you know where to find me. Promise me."

This earned a sympathetic grimace.

"Mr Holmes, there are things that I would rather tell *anyone* but you."

"Are you in trouble with the police?"

This remark scared Richard more than anything we had said in the meantime.

"Why do you think?"

"Because you were first headed to the precinct, were you not?"

First he blanched, then flushed and swallowed hard. A textbook example of a man who had been caught doing something he had not wanted to be spotted doing. But for the love of God I could not figure out what sinister occurrences may have compelled him to seek out the police.

Richard rebuffed our guesses.

"No, no, it's not like that," he said hurriedly, trying to divert attention from what we had seen a moment ago with our own eyes. "My people are having some problems with poachers, so I thought that constable Crusher might help them. But I changed my mind. They certainly have more important things to do."

Holmes's suspicion was not assuaged, but for now he accepted the explanation.

"I do not believe it," he smiled, opening his pocket watch to check the time.

We had been held up longer than we anticipated.

"Watson, we should go, our friends are waiting. By the way, Richard, I heard that your faculty finished second in the Eights this year. Congratulations."

"Thank you, sir. My muscles still ache," he said.

We shook his hand, which was cold with sweat. He was visibly relieved that the unexpected meeting was at an end. He bade us farewell and scampered away to disappear as quickly as possible from our sight.

Holmes and I walked in silence the short rest of the way to Dr Conway's as each of us analysed our feelings. There was no doubt that Richard Green was in some sort of trouble.

These concerns stayed with us the whole evening, especially Holmes, who played even worse than usual, and did not contribute much to the conversation. As expected, I drew him as my partner, and our opponents crushed us. Whittaker and Conway soon saw that the game did not hold much promise, so we finished earlier than usual and moved to the fireplace with a glass of brandy.

Even there, however, the thoughtful and frowning detective's tongue did not loosen.

Holmes was distracted, showed little interest in our conversation, and when our friends tried to involve him, dismissed them with abruptness bordering on rudeness. In this awkward atmosphere we chatted about local events, when the topic suddenly returned to Europe and escalating tensions on the continent.

"I still wonder, Holmes, that you took on those Germans, the Steiners," Conway suddenly said to the detective. "What made you do it?"

My friend, who cannot abide prejudice, levelled him with a steely gaze.

"Their references, of course," he said.

The poor doctor, an old country practitioner used to handling trivial injuries or illnesses did not have much experience with the corners of the human mind, let alone that of Holmes. He did not recognise when it was prudent to retreat, and instead of withdrawing, dug himself an even deeper hole.

"Nevertheless, you must admit that in the current situation it does not look proper."

Holmes put down his half-finished drink. Only someone who knew him as well as I did could see the inner storm and turmoil brewing behind the dangerously quiet tone. He never raised his voice.

"My dear Doctor, not only in Fulworth, but around the world life would be much better if we just rid ourselves of these prejudices."

Conway looked ashamed.

"I did not mean any harm," he said. "However, Germany recently launched a world war, and with whom they have elected Chancellor, you must admit there is reason for concern."

"My only concern is that the Chancellor's demagoguery does not spread to normal and sane people, among whom I still count you. There is no worse danger than when educated individuals allow themselves to be frightened by populist drivel."

"That's why people like the Steiners left Germany," the pastor added. "We cannot throw them all into one bag."

Before the debate could flare in a direction from which there was no returning, outside growled the engine of Steiner's car. The man who had unwittingly become the subject of our dispute had come to take us home.

We settled down in the back seat. When the lights of the village had disappeared behind us and the car headed to Cuckmere Haven, I broke the silence.

"You are not an ideal companion today," I chided.

"I am aware of that, my friend," he sighed. "Forgive me that last outburst."

"Did old Conway's words appal you so?"

"Oh, that does not bother me at all, my dear Watson," he said, waving his hand dismissively. "Next week he will be an expert on something else. He is a good-natured braggart, you know. I was just wondering why Richard lied to us."

So after all I was right.

"Lied? Do you think about his studies? He did seem odd to me. I think he did not want to upset you with the revelation of his poor marks."

"No, it is more than that," he said, shaking his head. "I fear that his problems are graver."

"What makes you think so?"

"His faculty did not finish second in the Eights, it finished third. If he still went to the school, he would know it, and would have realised that my question was a trick."

"Do you think they expelled him?" I asked. That would not have occurred to me.

"Perhaps. I will find out tomorrow," he said. "It would be a shame were he to throw away his talent, regardless of whether or not he is to blame."

"But you saw how upset he was. Second or third place, so what? I think it is about a girl. It may not be related to his studies at all!"

"Perhaps you are right," he said, scowling. "Better to sleep on it."

"I am sure that tomorrow he will come to explain everything himself," I said reassuringly.

But the next morning it was clear that Holmes had not slept much. When I went downstairs he was standing in his dressing gown, dishevelled and staring out the window at the driveway, where Steiner was raking the gravel in a herringbone pattern, as the detective liked it.

"It is still early for visitors," I said, guessing his thoughts. "Let's have some breakfast. Everything seems worse on an empty stomach. If he does not appear in the morning we will head to the village."

"Sometimes I should like to have a mind as carefree as yours," he grumbled, but allowed himself to be persuaded to change clothes and sit down for a hearty breakfast prepared for us by Mrs Steiner.

As the morning paper had not yet arrived, Holmes's turned his attention to his food and literally devoured the eggs, bacon and beans.

The Times arrived just in time for coffee, which Mrs Steiner brought to us in the winter garden.

In addition to papers there were also some pamphlets, a few letters and a beekeeping magazine, which Holmes snatched up first.

"Such a tragedy," said Mrs Steiner as she cleared the table.

"Pardon me?" Holmes said, blinking over the top of his magazine.

"Don't even ask, Mr Holmes," she lamented. "The postman said that a dead body was found. A poor man hanged himself at the Three Oaks."

A chill ran down my spine.

"Who is it?"

"He did not say. He did not know. The constable was just there a moment ago."

"You do not think..." I said, looking at the detective.

But I did not even finish my sentence.

He jumped up, threw down the magazine, almost knocked over the housekeeper and dashed into the driveway, where Steiner was preparing to wash the car. He scattered the landscaped path, hastily overturned the bucket of water and sat behind the wheel. He had not driven in years and in this excited state I could not let him go alone. I hurried after him, trying not to suspect the worst.

Unfortunately, it was true.

Richard Green had hanged himself.

* Dr Watson has been married several times, although it is not clear whether two or three times. His first wife was Mary Morstan, to whom he became engaged in the novel *The Sign of Four*. After her death he married at least once more, but the records are not clear. Details of other marriages are not known.

** The tragic circumstances of Holmes's early retirement are recounted in the novel *Golem's Shadow: The Fall of Sherlock Holmes*.

*** Dr Fu Manchu was a brilliant Chinese scientist and criminal mastermind created by English author Sax Rohmer. It is not clear under what circumstances and when Holmes confronted the greatest criminal mind of the Far East.

**** Pastor Barlow tried to induce a fatal heart attack in Holmes using tobacco mixed with digitalis – see *The Adventure of the Cold-served Revenge*.

***** A bee smoker is a canister with a nozzle at the end of a small bellows, fanning the smoke. It is used to calm bees.

III

At the Three Oaks

The Three Oaks was the name of a small grove on a hill behind Fulworth farther away from the coast. In addition to the road that went through the forest towards Eastbourne, it could also be reached from the village by a footpath lined with shrubs and bushes, ending at a small chapel. This place of pilgrimage was chosen by Richard as the venue for his voluntary departure from the world. The report on the tragedy had spread, and when we arrived, the first curious onlookers had begun to converge. The local police had arrived and started to do their work just before us. The grief-stricken Holmes this time did not interfere with their duties.

Young Green hung from a thick branch on the lower third of a mighty tree. On the grass beneath him lay a few fragments of bark and his left shoe. Never in my notes had I ever described the condition of a body that had suffered such a death, moreover of someone who was close to me, so forgive me if it is not the most detailed account.

It was a truly horrible sight.

Richard's once handsome face was livid with colour, the features mutilated beyond recognition by posthumous convulsions. His swollen purple tongue stuck out from his mouth pinched between his teeth. His eyes were open wide and blood trickled from his nose. The skin of his neck was cut by the noose, made of the kind of rope that can be found on every country farm.

There was no doubt about the cause of death. Richard obviously knew what he was doing. The loop was tied neatly and the rope was long enough to ensure death without torment. Death had been immediate and irreversible, even had it been discovered early and someone had attempted a rescue. According to the colour of the skin, however, I concluded that he had died in the middle of the night, so there was little chance that anyone would have been around to prevent the tragedy.

Holmes was gasping, partly from shock, but also from physical exertion. In his haste he had forgotten his age and now leaned on me for support. I felt him stagger and offered my arm.

"I will never understand this," said Constable Crusher, who approached us without a greeting.

The constable was much younger than Holmes and I, but still old enough to know Richard from childhood and the detective's relationship with him. His feelings must have been similar to ours.

The detective nodded.

"May I help you in any way?" he asked.

"With all due respect, I do not think so, Mr Holmes," said Crusher. "As you see for yourself, foul play can be ruled out. This is a clear case of suicide. The paperwork for this unfortunate event will take longer than the investigation. I can only imagine why he did it."

"You can imagine, I intend to learn the truth," said Holmes.

The constable cleared his throat and sighed, launching a cloud of steam into the cool morning air. The last thing he wanted was to engage in a verbal exchange.

"Did he leave a note?"

"We have not found one, no."

"And you searched him?"

Crusher blinked.

"Well, I did not give a specific order to do so, but if he stayed here..."

He did not finish his sentence, and in order to avoid a lecture by the detective on the proper methodology for the investigation of a presumed suicide, he turned to his men and barked some orders at them.

Holmes meanwhile walked several painful steps closer to the crime scene. None of the younger officers dared drive him away. The onlookers from the village kept a respectful distance. The detective carefully walked around the body, looked at the surrounding land, and then threw his head back and looked up into the branches where he studied something for a moment.

He touched the trunk of the tree with his finger and shook his head helplessly.

"I must agree with you, Constable," he said quietly. "Besides your men, no one else was here in the last hours. Richard came alone, climbed the tree, and brought about his own death."

I had to take a handkerchief out of my pocket and hold it in front of my nose and mouth. The longer we stayed at the site, the more intense the odour became. The young man, or rather his body, had expelled all of its fluids, which were now slowly drying on his legs.

"There are fragments of bark under his fingernails, scratches on the branches where he tied the rope, and traces on the trunk of the tree where he climbed," said the detective. "Nobody helped him or compelled him to do this."

The pitying tone in which he pronounced his assessment was nothing other than a desire to find a rational explanation for a death that seemed so senseless. He was able to fight crime, to punish it; but the motive for the suicide, regardless of its justification, remained only a motive. Nothing would change the fact that the young boy had voluntarily taken his own life instead of fighting for it.

"And so as not to do you an injustice," he continued, "it is clear that he did not leave a suicide note. If he had, he would have left it somewhere where we could find it."

Crusher nodded, but I saw that he was unsure of himself in Holmes's presence. My friend's aura of authority had affected all police officers thus for decades.

"Dr Conway is still on his way," the constable said. "The time of death has not yet been determined. I'll ask around the village for where he was last seen. My guess would be around midnight. It is the most common time for suicides."

Holmes looked at me and I shook my head.

"Death came in the early morning hours," I said. "It is evident by the fresh smell. The body defecated in the last three or four hours."

I took out my pocket watch. Holmes and I were in the habit of rising quite early, even at our age, awoken by the morning light. It was now shortly after nine o'clock in the morning. The postman, who had brought the message, came on weekdays around eight. The body therefore could have been found around seven, which indeed Crusher confirmed. I estimated the time of death at around five o'clock in the morning, shortly before dawn, which at this time of year was around half past five.

The loud chatter of the curious onlookers hungry for sensation pulled me out of my musings.

"Has someone informed Mr Green's parents?"

Crusher realised where I was going. He pushed his hat back and scratched his ear awkwardly.

"I have not sent anyone yet. We only identified the body shortly before your arrival."

"I understand," said Holmes. "But now we must hurry. I would not wish them to hear the news from some stranger. It is so cruel."

"I'll go there," said the constable.

"It is better if you stay here," said the detective, stopping him. "See, please, that Richard's body is inspected and brought to the morgue as soon as possible. I do not want this theatre to last longer than absolutely necessary."

He turned for the last time and looked sadly into the dead eyes of his protégé. Such wasted intellect, talent, ambition and dreams!

"I will go to the Greens myself," he said to the constable. "Come, Watson, you will drive."

***

We sat on a wooden bench in the kitchen of Richard's parents' house, waiting for his mother's sobbing to subside. Her body shook with hysterical sobs, while Richard's father just stared blankly out the window into the fields.

On the walls there were pictures of Richard, probably from about five years ago, before he went to London. I will always remember how he looked then, his boyish features and bright brown eyes somehow incongruous with the athletic and virile rower's body.

Mr Greene could no longer fight the onslaught of tears and cried out in pain. The sound broke through the silence like a shot and I jumped in surprise. His crying also interrupted Mrs Green.

"Had he confided in you about any problems or why he might have done what he did?" Holmes asked.

The boy's father turned ponderously from the window. After the initial shock, when we feared they might collapse, the parents began to evince other emotions. For Mr Green it was anger. Not directed at us, but at Richard and the solution he had chosen. It was a common psychological reaction to the passing of a loved one. His already careworn face with its greying, well-kept beard seemed to become even more lined with despair.

"Why?" he cried. "Because he was a coward! Whatever happened, he had to face it like a man! He has dishonoured his whole family!"

His eyes darkened with a mixture of sorrow and helplessness. Then he suddenly banged his fist on the table, snorted angrily and stormed out the door, slamming it behind him.

Ms Green again wept, but the hysteria had subsided.

I took her hand to soothe her, as her husband should have done. But he had to deal with his grief in his own way. She took it and held it tightly.

"Yesterday I met him briefly in the village and I immediately could see that something had happened," said Holmes.

Green wiped her swollen eyes filled with tears.

"He came home two days ago," she wailed. "He said he needed to clear his head... to think about something... and that he could not concentrate in London. He said he needed distance. But he did not say what the matter was. He did not want to talk about it. Poor boy, if only I knew..."

"He said the same to me," Holmes nodded. "But he would not reveal his problems at school or anything else."

"Did he have a lady friend?" I asked.

"He did," she said. "When he was home last Christmas he spoke a lot about her. He said that when he was sure she was the right one he would bring her to us... In his last letter he wrote they would come together in the summer."

At the thought her chin again began to tremble.

"How old is this letter?"

"No more than two weeks," she said wearily.

"Was there something else that might indicate what was bothering him?" he asked.

"No, not really... That's why I was surprised when he arrived and was so out of sorts."

"Whatever happened to him had to have happened in the last days," said Holmes. "Perhaps the girl will know. Do you know her name?"

"No," she said, blowing her nose in her apron. "He did not mention her name."

"Strange. May I see that last letter?"

The grief-stricken woman shuffled toward a large trunk and took out a small wooden box, in which she saved her son's letters. At the top, still in the envelope, was the most recent one. She showed it to the curious detective.

"The return address is a private flat in London," he said. "I thought that Richard had rooms at the university?"

"He recently moved. He said he found something, because of that girl. He had gotten a job somewhere, in a laboratory, I think. He explained it to me, but I'm just a simple woman. I do not understand these things."

Holmes quickly read the letter and handed it to me. The note was hardly worth mentioning. The typical letter from a student to his rural parents, meant to allay their fears about the sinfulness of the city. In it he mentioned meeting a decent girl from a good family, whom he promised to introduce at the earliest opportunity.

"You are entirely blameless, Mrs Green," I said, returning her the letter.

"What led Richard to such a desperate act is a mystery to us all," said Holmes. "He obviously did not want our help. And when he judged a solution to be beyond his power, he chose the worst way out."

"I will be haunted to my death by the idea of the terrible thing that must have happened to him!"

The detective did not want to upset her even more. But he still needed some answers.

"Would you permit me to look in his room?" he asked gently.

She consented and led us feebly to the second floor of the simple house, where we were let into a small room. Richard had grown up here, and after his departure for London the parents had not changed anything in the room. He stayed there whenever he returned home. On the shelves was the dusty equipment of an amateur chemist, used in his first childhood experiments under the supervision of Holmes, several books, textbooks and other small items.

Behind the door there was an open suitcase. It contained nothing but a few pieces of clothing, all of which indicated only that the young man had planned to spend about a week in Fulworth. Again there was no suicide note. We found nothing to suggest that his death had been planned ahead of time.

The spring sun peered through the half open shutters, illuminating the white linen of the bed, which no one had slept in last night.

"Did it not strike you as odd that Richard did not come home last night?"

"No, Mr Holmes," she said, squeezing a corner of her apron. "He said that he was seeing his friends. I thought they were getting drunk together. You know, it was not his style, but I was hoping that it would help cheer him up."

"I understand. I'll ask if he met someone," he said, nodding and turning to leave, when he noticed something else in the suitcase. Among the shirts there was a photograph. Holmes pulled it out into the light to get a better look at it. It was of a very graceful blonde-haired girl with a small, symmetrical face and a modern hairstyle. I guessed she was a little older than Richard, but not by much, nothing that might attract scandal.

"I assume this is the girl," said the detective.

"The poor dear," said Mrs Green, looking regretfully at the image of her son's sweetheart. She patted the photograph and hugged it to her heart. "It will also be a shock for her. Who will tell her? And how? We do not even know her name!"

"Do not worry about that now. I will find her and handle this matter," Holmes said.

We returned with the sobbing mother to the sitting room and made ready to depart.

"Mrs Green, you said that Richard had taken a job to make some extra money for his studies, but I suspect that perhaps he had left the university. The move away from the campus implies it. Would you happen to know anything about it?"

"Indeed not!" she said, so horrified that she forgot to cry. "Oh dear, we spent all of our savings on his studies!"

"I know," said Holmes nodding, "I know. Perhaps I am mistaken. I assure you that I shall find out. We cannot bring the boy back to life, but we deserve an explanation."

Richard obviously was not just keeping a secret from Holmes, but also from his parents.

"Please, do not tell my husband of your suspicions, he would not survive it," she begged us. "Richard's education and career was his purpose in life. I do not believe Richard could have disappointed us so. Oh God!"

"I shall not presume anything until the whole matter is resolved," Holmes promised. "Tell me one last thing. Do you have trouble with poachers?"

"Not at all," she said. "What gave you that idea?"

"I just heard something," said the detective. "And now we will not bother you any longer. I am immensely sorry for your loss. I did not think that in the twilight of my life I would have to deal with such a task."

She bade us farewell and again broke into tears. As we went out be met old Mr Green, who had cooled down and come to mourn with his wife.

We left the farm with many questions and only a few answers. But Holmes had made a promise, to the Greens and to himself, so I was certain he would not rest until it was fulfilled. And he could be just as certain that I would follow him.

On the way from Richard's parents we stopped at the police station.

"It is now clear beyond a shadow of doubt that what weighed on Richard was criminal in nature," said Holmes thoughtfully as we parked back in the village near the benches, where yesterday the case had begun.

"I would still not rule out the possibility that the girl played a role in this," I countered. "Perhaps it was a way to escape a broken heart. You know how vulnerable young people are. And his wild reaction when I mentioned the possibility yesterday."

"With all due respect, Watson, that is utter nonsense."

"How so?"

"Why, the absence of a suicide note, after all," he exclaimed, as if it were the most obvious thing in the world. "If you took your own life due to unrequited love you would certainly want the object of your love to know it. Scream your pain and heartbreak to the world! No, Watson, Richard died precisely because he had a secret that he did *not* want anyone to know."

"Perhaps he did not leave a note because his decision was a spontaneous one."

"No, believe me; the girl is not behind it. He was ashamed of something. His conscience was weighed down by a burden, one so heavy that he could not confide either in his parents or in me."

"I did not think about it that way," I admitted.

"And then his last journey here, to the police station," he continued as we climbed the stairs to Constable Crusher's office. "I do not think he actually would have confessed to something had we not met him and scared him off, but I cannot help feeling guilty that this may have been the case."

Richard's story that he had wanted to ask the constable for help with poachers was clearly a fiction, even had his mother not denied it today.

What could the young man have been implicated in?

The constable confounded us even more. When we sat down in front of his desk to recount the visit to Richard's parents, he told us that the examination of the young man's body had raised more questions than answers.

"In the boy's pockets we found a fortune," he said.

"Excellent!" cried Holmes. "No doubt some clues!"

"I do not mean in the figurative sense," said the policeman. "But an actual fortune!"

So saying he took from a drawer a stack of folded bills, at first glance clearly a few hundred pounds. It had been folded in Richard's jacket pocket.

Holmes furrowed his brow. I realised that if we wanted to know the truth about what his protégé was involved in in London, the time had come to return to our old stomping grounds.

IV

Porton Down

That afternoon we boarded a train, but before we did, we spent the rest of the day walking around Fulworth, trying to reconstruct the last hours of Richard's life. From his local acquaintances, among whom he never quite fit in due to his intelligence and ambition, and whom he had met the evening before, we learned that he did not head home after our encounter in front of the police station. That evening he had been seen in the local pub, where he drank slowly, but sought neither company nor conversation. Indeed, under the influence of alcohol his dejection was all the greater than when sober, and he drove away anyone who approached him. When he left before midnight he was only a shadow.

The innkeeper said that he had been taken aback when Richard paid with a banknote of unusually high value, but did not think twice about it. Guests with money are better than those with none. For Holmes, the wad of banknotes found on the young man was another piece of the puzzle pointing to something suspicious. On the train we discussed ways he could have come by such a sum. Despite our efforts we could not find many honest ways.

The least serious was gambling.

"He certainly could have won such a sum at cards, dice or some other such game of chance, though such a win would call into question the motive for suicide," I said.

"You have to look at things from different angles, not just those that suggest themselves," said Holmes. "He may have owed much more than he won. Surely you can imagine the pressure that moneylenders can exert..."

He was right, as always.

Nevertheless, another possibility occurred to me, though I hesitated to bring it up. Richard's study of chemistry suggested that he may have been involved in the growing trade in illegal opiates. It was no secret that there was a lot of money to be made in this business. A brilliant chemist like young Green was extremely valuable for the criminal organisations involved in this trade and could have explained the wad of banknotes in his pocket. Holmes, himself once an avid user of cocaine, knew first-hand the hazards of opiate addiction and its tragic consequences.*

That was why I did not want to raise this issue just yet. I feared that under the pressure of recent circumstances he might suffer a relapse.

But now the challenge of tackling a new case seemed to reinvigorate him.

Upon arriving in London, we booked a room at a guesthouse near our former residence in Baker Street, ate a quick dinner and went straight to bed in order to gain strength for the next day. We expected it would be a difficult one.

There were two places where we could begin the investigation: Richard's university or his flat, the address of which we knew from the envelope of the letter to his mother, and to which we had a key, thanks to the good constable, who had found it in Richard's pocket, and grudgingly lent it to my friend, off the record of course.

The detective, however, decided to start at the university. He wanted to talk to Richard's teachers and classmates, and the surest way to reach them was in the morning. Once lectures ended we would only be able to find them with difficulty.

The dormitories of University College London occupied land outside the city centre, but the chemical department of the Mathematics and Physics Faculty was located on Gordon Street. We went there in the early morning, arranging with the cab driver to be on hand throughout the day, naturally for a very generous amount of money.

University College London was founded in 1826 and was the first in England to open its gates to women. For this reason, the detective hoped that perhaps Richard's lady friend would be among the students and that his classmates would identify her for us.

But to our surprise, nobody proffered any information about her. At first I thought perhaps they were put off by two old men inquiring into the private life of a fellow student, but with every successive blank face I suspected that something else lay behind it. After half a dozen futile inquiries, we came across a female student who was aware of Holmes's somewhat tarnished fame, and was more willing to provide some basic information.

At least until we explained to her who we were looking for and why.

She puckered her rather plain face in a disapproving grimace, as though she had just received a bad mark on a chemistry test.

"Richard was always special, but he was no sissy," she said thoughtfully.

"We're looking for his lady friend," said Holmes. "It is our sad duty to tell her about Richard's fate. And I also believe it will help us clarify his motive."

"I recall him talking about a girl a few months ago," she said. "He said they went to the cinema together. I remember because it was the new Chaplin film, *Modern Times* I think. Have you seen it? I laughed terribly when he described some of the scenes. Sometimes we exchanged a few words in class; I sat next to him at lectures whenever there was a test."

She smiled guiltily when saying this and the detective seemed pleased to learn that his protégé was a student whose work was copied by others.

As the school building was quickly emptying before the next lecture, Holmes did not waste more time.

"Is she a student?" he asked. "Do you know where I can find her?"

"I'm afraid I have no idea, she was not a student," she said, walking to the door of the lecture hall. "I understood that she was from a good family and was a little older, but that's all I remember, I'm sorry."

"When did you last speak to him?"

"It's been a few months. We weren't friends or anything like that. And I'm not exactly the most popular girl in school. Richard let me copy from him, because I helped him with Professor Biggles's class, but that's all."

"Why did you stop talking with him?"

She opened the door of the lecture hall and looked back at us before entering.

"Because he hasn't been at school since," she said. "Now if you'll excuse me."

The lecture was just about to start, and the infirm, white-haired professor who was to deliver it aimed a look at us indicating that no delay would be permitted. We closed the door. But we had no joy in the fact that Holmes's instinct had been correct. Why had Green left school? It did not seem to fit.

By now we had already begun to attract attention.

"Gentlemen, may I help you?" said a stern man of our age approaching us. He was dressed in academic robes and blinked at us through thick horn-rimmed glasses. "May I remind you that consultations with parents are only by appointment?"

"You must be Dean Marbury!" said Holmes proffering his hand. "I no longer follow the field as closely as I once did, but I knew your predecessor well."

"With whom do I have the honour?"

"Oh, pardon my rudeness. My name is Sherlock Holmes, and this is my associate, Dr Watson," the detective said.

"But of course!" the professor cried, aware of my friend's reputation. And not only as a criminologist, but also the reputation he enjoyed in scientific circles. The detective's passion for the natural sciences was well known and few disciplines fascinated him as much as chemistry. I well remember his experiments in our lodgings at Baker Street, some of which ended with damage to Mrs Hudson's fittings and furnishings. But I never ceased to wonder at Holmes's encyclopaedic knowledge of substances, poisons and all manner of bizarre chemicals as well as his ability to classify and draw inferences from them to answer the thorniest mysteries.

Marbury invited us into his office, where he took off his academic robes and offered us a cup of coffee. He and Holmes lit their pipes, while I settled for a cigar.

"To what do I owe the pleasure of this visit?" the Dean asked after we had exchanged a few good-natured remarks, in which he and the detective discussed mutual acquaintances.

"You may remember that some years ago I sent you a letter of recommendation for a student," said Holmes. "Today I am here again because of him."

"Yes, of course," he said. "Though I must confess I do not recall the student's name..."

"Richard Green," I said.

"Ah yes, Mr Green," said Marbury, but even as poor an observer as I could not miss the change in the professor's expression that he tried quickly to disguise. "However, you will no longer find him with us. No doubt the students have already told you..."

"I am aware of that," said the detective, puffing on his pipe. "His body is currently lying in the morgue in Fulworth and his family is preparing the funeral."

"Oh my God!" the Dean cried, jumping from his chair. "What happened? How did he die?"

Holmes folded his fingers and scrutinised Marbury with his hawk-like eyes.

"Suicide," he said calmly.

The professor rubbed the bridge of his nose and took a deep breath, as if he wanted to ask something, but then thought better of it. Instead, he wordlessly extinguished his pipe, poured the ashes into a wastebasket and sipped his coffee. The clink of the china saucer when he returned the empty cup was like a bell announcing the end of the meeting. Our time was up faster than we had hoped.

"Why do I feel that pronouncing Richard's name makes people lock their mouths?" asked the detective.

"I truly cannot tell you," said the professor. "Know, however, that this wasted life fills my soul with sadness. He was one of the best minds to have passed through this faculty."

"Why, then, did he quit his studies? And when? Did you talk with him about it? Did somebody compel him to do it?"

Marbury opened the office door and politely, but insistently, urged us to leave.

"If I could be of service in anything at all, in the field of chemistry for example, my knowledge is available to you. But on this topic I cannot say a word."

I got up stiffly to leave, but my friend remained seated.

"I have taken upon myself the responsibility of clarifying the reason for his death," he said, crossing one leg over the other and brushing away an invisible speck. "Besides your school I have no other clues."

"Really I do not see how I can help," the professor insisted. "It would be sheer folly were I to get involved. At the end of the semester I am going to retire. Please understand; I am bound to secrecy."

"Get involved in what?"

"In what Mr Green was involved in. But you, Mr Holmes, with your relationships and contacts at the highest level, will certainly find him yourself. That is all I can suggest. And now, please..."

"Thank you for your time and for the coffee," the detective said coldly, rising from the chair. "I believe that when I learn what I need to know I will understand your caution."

With these words we left the churlish academic in his barren office and returned to the cab that was waiting for us in front of the university. The spring sun had emerged, but the car was still pleasantly cool.

Holmes told the driver to go to the address of Richard's flat, where we intended to continue the search. Then, as was his habit, Holmes confided his observations to me.

"The key to everything, my dear Watson, was Marbury's last remark."

"About your contacts in government circles?"

"Exactly, my friend," he said. "Alas I can no longer turn to brother Mycroft. How much easier our quest would have been! Perhaps we will find more clues in Richard's flat. However, if it is as I suspect, everything will change completely."

The second part of Holmes' habit of confiding in me was to suggest mysteries about to be unravelled while leaving me hanging in the air without an answer. But in addition to wrinkles, my many years had given me experience and patience, so I did bother to extract more information from him and instead settled into my seat for the ride. We rattled through the whole of London, so I had a chance again to explore the growing and changing city, pulsating with lively traffic. I realised how little I missed it. I was happy in rural Fulworth, and everything that I had liked best in London was long gone.

Richard's flat was on the second floor of a nice, relatively new house on the other side of town. It was not exactly the periphery, more a suburban area, home mostly to the lower middle classes. The house unfortunately had no elevator, so we had to climb quite a few steep stairs.

Holmes unlocked the door and we entered into a surprisingly nicely furnished room, which adjoined another smaller bedroom and bathroom. The living area had a kitchenette with a tin stove.

Nobody was there. I do not know why that surprised me.

At first glance Richard's flat gave the impression of a refuge for an oppressed student who was standing on his own feet and beginning to prosper. The furnishings were a mixture of older things and a few new more expensive-looking pieces. A number of details, such as the curtains and the well-equipped kitchen, suggested a woman's touch. In the air hung the still fresh scent of women's perfume.

The detective looked in the bathroom and bedroom. Over his shoulder I saw an open closet full of menswear carefully hung on hangers or folded into piles. A few were scattered about, as Richard hurriedly packed for his final journey home. On the made bed there was the imprint of a heavy trunk. On the nightstand there was a photograph of Richard and the young lady, whom we already knew from the picture in Fulworth.

"There are women's things in the bathroom and in the closet, but only a few pieces. Richard's lady friend was certainly a frequent guest, but they did not live together," said Holmes. "Unfortunately, she continues to slip through our fingers."

On the bedside table there was more than just the photograph. The detective tensed, practically bounded over the varnished parquet floor, and grabbed some kind of identification card. He studied it, turned to me and raised his hand, holding it aloft triumphantly as though it were the Holy Grail.

"Eureka!" he exclaimed. "This is the first crucial piece of our jigsaw puzzle!"

"What is it?"

"A pass to Porton Down! Look!"

Indeed it was. The leather case contained a rectangle of hard cardboard with a stamped photograph, Richard's initials and signature, entitling the holder to enter this facility.

"But what is at Porton Down?" I asked. "I've never heard of the place."

"It seems our security forces are doing something well after all," Holmes replied mysteriously. "If Richard was part of what was happening there, I am not surprised that Marbury was so close-lipped. I quite understand his fears and anxieties as well as his final remark. Porton Down is a secret government science facility near Salisbury."

"A government science facility?" I asked. "Secret?"

"Precisely," Holmes nodded. "That helps answer a lot of questions. Apparently Richard left school not because he was not good enough, but because he was *too* good. His shining talent must have caught the attention of someone important, indeed to the point where His Majesty's

Government called upon him even before he had completed his education. But this just raises so many more questions. What was so secret that neither he nor his professors could speak about it?"

"And more importantly, if it is related to his suicide," I added.

"That is undoubtedly a good question, my dear Watson," he said. "However not *if*, but *how*?"

*See *Golem's Shadow: The Fall of Sherlock Holmes*

V.

Bacillus Anthracis

Holmes sat on the edge of Richard's bed and stared at the pass to Porton Down. My friend was not the kind of man who readily showed his emotions. His brain favoured rational analysis over tragic outbursts, and with the exception of his suffering from the effects of withdrawal, I have never seen him lose control over his feelings. Now, however, I was sure that somewhere deep inside him, behind the glassy stare, was a storm.

Since the discovery of the young man's body he had practically had no time to cope with the tragedy. He had to be strong in front of his parents, in front of the constable, indeed even in front of me. And I felt his sorrow over the clues suggesting that his protégé had dropped out of school. Now that he knew that he had been wronged, and that Richard had not disappointed, he was partially relieved. I let him grieve and silently returned to the living room.

I parted the curtains and opened the window to let in some fresh air. It smelled like spring, not the fresh rural kind, but the London kind, mingled scents whose description would require many pages to describe. The view from the flat was of the brick wall of the house opposite and a small, grassy backyard.

I reflected for a moment about the significance of our discovery. There could only be one reason for the connection between a leading chemist like Richard and a top-secret government project scientist. And like the old soldier that I was, I could not be pleased. I had experienced the horrors of the Boer War; in Afghanistan I had learned of man's barbarousness to man, the brutal instruments of war, the bow and the spear. And that was without the sophistication of chemistry.

I was jerked out of these contemplations by a rustling noise behind me. Holmes was on his feet, carefully searching the room.

He started with the cupboards and drawers in the kitchenette and continued with the racks above them. He paused at the stove. In the trash bin he found an empty canvas board without labelling. For a moment he turned it over in his hands; and then he knelt and opened the door of the oven.

"What did you find?" I asked.

"Nothing yet," he said, squinting into the darkness inside. "In those panels there had to be something. Something that Richard decided to burn. Please give me a tray or some sort of container."

I took a tray from one of the kitchen cabinets, and Holmes dug out the cigarette butts and ashes from the stove. A breeze blew in from the open window, kicking up a roiling ash cloud and enveloping the room in a greyish haze. By the time I closed the window and the ashes subsided it was too late. The furniture as well as our clothing and faces were covered. Only our hair did not change colour. We had been grey with age for many years now.

But the detective did not mind. He carefully sifted through the ashes on the tray, in which he gathered larger embers that had not burned completely. On two pieces letters were legible, but by themselves they did not make much sense.

I helped Holmes to his feet and we sat down at the dusty table to get a better look at the charred bits of papers. So that they would not disintegrate under our clumsy fingers, we used wooden toothpicks as makeshift tweezers. As luck would have it, the detective, probably from old habit, was carrying his magnifying glass. After focusing intently for a while from a distance of several inches, he managed to put together two words, or rather, one word and one punctuation mark.

"I am almost certain that I am able to identify the word *pastor* here", he said, carefully showing me the blackened paper. "It is no doubt a name, however, as it begins with a capital letter and is not at the beginning of a sentence. In front of it I can even identify the previous letter *n* and there is a period visible between them. It is also possible that this is only part of a longer name, because the line does not seem to finish here."

I trusted that his eyesight was better than mine. Although I could barely make out tiny pen strokes in the embers, I could not discern any letters. Holmes pulled a small notebook out of his pocket and wrote down the word *Pastor*. He also wrote other variations of names, such as Pastoria, Pastorius and others. He paid no more attention to the tiny cinder and it disintegrated into a fine powder.

The detective redirected his attention to the second piece of paper.

"Here the mark LZ 129 is clearly visible," he said.

"Does that mean anything?"

"Absolutely nothing," he said, leaning back in the chair.

"Could it be a chemical compound or element?"

"If it is, I am not aware of it," he said, frowning and absently tapping the bone handle of the magnifying glass on the table. "But I cannot rule it out. It is of course possible that in Porton Down a new element has been discovered and is being worked with. So far, however, an element with such a high atomic number is unheard of."

"Shall we wait here for the girl?" I suggested.

Interviewing her seemed like the logical next step. So far everything we had was just baseless speculation.

"My friend, one does not wait for answers, they rarely come by themselves," said Holmes. "No, we must seek them out. However, we know exactly where to look!"

He placed the pass to Porton Down, the magnifying glass and the notebook in his pocket and stood up to leave. I had to concede that I had hoped we would wait in the flat for the girl, because raindrops had begun drumming on the windowsill and I would rather wait in a dry place.

"There is an umbrella at the bottom of the cabinet," Holmes said, as though reading my mind. "I gather Richard shall not object if we borrow it."

But as I pulled the umbrella out of the cabinet, it latched onto a wire beside it, which triggered the door of a secret compartment to open.

I have seen a lot of money in my life, but rarely so much in one place.

"Holmes, you have to see this!" I called to the detective.

He looked unhappily at the wads of banknotes, which were carefully stacked in a case. If the amount found on Green by Constable Crusher was suspicious, what lay in the case practically screamed criminal wrongdoing. I estimated the total at around fifty thousand pounds. The government was certainly not *that* generous with its experts.

The detective did not comment. He removed the case from the closet, blew the ashes out of his hat, put it on his head and went back to the waiting car. Outside, Holmes and I exchanged the umbrella, and when I sat in the car, he handed me the case with the money. He himself did not enter to car, but remained on the sidewalk.

"You're not coming?" I asked.

"I have an errand, Watson," he said, and gave me a few instructions. "First go to the bank and rent a safety deposit box for the money. Then call Cuckmere Haven and tell Mrs Steiner that we will likely stay in the city a long time. Ask her to tell Mr Steiner to drive down with some clothes for us. Ideally tomorrow; another pair of hands will surely be of use to us."

Then he slammed the door of the car, tapped on the roof and let me go.

I did not see him again until evening. I spent the rest of the afternoon outside. According to his instructions, I put the money in the bank, where I waited for over an hour in order to arrange the requisite paperwork.

When he returned, he did not want to talk much about the case. He told me that he was exhausted and needed to compare the facts in his head. Without revealing too many details, he informed me that he had spent the rest of the day talking with his dusty old contacts in the ministries of the interior and defence.

He only wanted a light dinner, but once he had eaten his tongue loosened somewhat. Before we adjourned to our room, we had brandy in the lobby of our guesthouse, as was our custom at home. Between sips Holmes and I discussed the other things that lay heavily on his heart. He confirmed that behind Richard's tragic suicide was a plot that went far beyond what we could have initially suspected.

"I met with several people today, and when I told them that my investigation was leading to Porton Down, their reaction was akin to Professor Marbury's. There is no doubt that the secret service and the military are in the game. In today's dangerous political climate, I must therefore ask you if you wish to continue the investigation."

I had never hesitated to follow my friend into battle before. And despite my advanced age, nothing had changed in that regard. My revolver was clean and at the ready. I said as much to Holmes, who smiled and squeezed my shoulder. Satisfied, he went into the room.

In the morning there were two surprises waiting for us in the lobby of the guesthouse. The first was that good Major Steiner had come together with his wife. The detective raised his eyebrows when he saw her, but said nothing. He knew our housekeeper well enough to understand that her husband did not have much choice in the matter. If she had decided that she should be present, there was no force on earth that could stop her.

The second surprise was a sealed envelope, brought early in the morning by a courier, who had left it at reception. It was addressed to Sherlock Holmes. I noted the name of the sender, but I cannot reveal it here. The man is still politically active and I do not wish to thwart his ambitions by mentioning him here. The envelope contained two passes, clearly issued in secret at the highest levels, and a brief letter.

The detective read it quickly and handed one of the passes to me. It was the same pass that we had found in Green's flat, but with our photographs. They entitled us to enter the laboratory facility at Porton Down.

"It is gratifying to know that my service to the Crown is still appreciated," he said. "Naturally, the debt owed me by one government official has now been paid. By the way, I took your photograph from an old article in *The Strand* – I trust you will not mind."

Indeed, I did not. Quite the contrary, actually, as in the photograph I still had my dark hair.

"Unfortunately I did not obtain a pass for you, my dear Steiner," he said to our driver. "According to my contact, I failed to dispel fears about your nationality. Germans are not welcome in the lab. We will have to travel alone, Watson."

The Steiners did not seem perturbed. Mrs Steiner especially welcomed the possibility of a free day in the city, which she rarely had. The major took Holmes aside for a brief word in private and then we left them to their own affairs.

Without further delay, we embarked on a hundred-mile journey to the mysterious region near Salisbury in the county of Wiltshire.

As we neared our destination, there began to appear the first signs that we were entering a highly sensitive area. The road was lined with signs warning of the dangers ahead and to ready our documents for inspection. This occurred at a sentry box before the front gate, which Holmes pulled up to after almost three hours of driving.

The officer at the gate looked at us closely and rigorously examined our passes. Then he saluted.

"You are expected, sir," he said, handing the documents back to the detective and pointing to a nearby building, in front of which was a parking lot. "You can park over there; the Lieutenant will pick you up."

We drove into an area bounded by a high fence with barbed wire, behind which could be seen a few low-rise buildings – laboratories, halls, warehouses and barracks. In the parking lot there were several other civilian vehicles, and to my astonishment I also saw fenced pastures containing sheep, goats, horses and cows.

"The facility has an area of almost seven thousand acres," Holmes said. "I studied it yesterday afternoon. One must learn about the lions' den before entering it."

He handed me one of the numbered clip cards saying *Visitor* on it that we had been given at the gate.

While he parked, he briefly recounted the history of this military and scientific facility.

Porton Down had been founded in March 1916 at the height of the Great War as Britain's answer to Germany's experiments with chemical weapons. The laboratories were tasked with secretly developing and testing chlorine, phosgene and mustard gas, a dangerous nerve gas, primarily in order to find an effective defence against them. And so it was today. The entire facility employed dozens of civilian scientists and an army of other workers, including soldiers protecting the top secret results.

A young lieutenant was waiting for us at the door and led us inside.

"Who are we supposed to meet?" I asked Holmes.

"The person in charge here is Dr Paul Fildes, at least as regards the scientific purpose of the facility," he said. "My contact at the ministry made us an appointment."

The lieutenant showed us to a modest office, whose walls were lined with metal filing cabinets and a blackboard covered with chalk markings. Dr Fildes was just in the process of erasing it with a dry sponge. If he did so for security reasons, he need not have bothered. The bits of formulas that I saw may have been in Swahili for all I could decipher of them.

Fildes's appearance corresponded to the world of academia from which he hailed, although the detective whispered to me just before we entered that he had formerly had a career in the Royal Navy. Indeed, he seemed to match the best of both worlds. A tall, upright posture of military bearing, dressed in the typical professor's tweed suit with waistcoat and white collared shirt. His cravat was tied carelessly; apparently he had hardly slept last night. A round nose protruded from his fifty-year-old face, bordered with trimmed greying hair beneath a shiny bald head.

"I must admit, Mr Holmes, that I was surprised when command informed me of your arrival," he said, motioning us to uncomfortable metal chairs in front of his desk. "But then I realised that your profession knows no terms like retirement or rest. I have followed most of your cases, so I am pleased that you have taken an interest in this sensitive matter."

Given that Holmes had as yet not revealed the purpose of our visit, Fildes's confession surprised him. The detective had not shared any details with his contact at the ministry, and except for the local newspapers, there had been no mention of Richard's suicide in the media. The case was too insignificant.

"Perhaps I should bring you up to speed...," said Fildes. "As you know, the situation in Europe is not exactly rosy, and there is a real danger that chaos may come again. Britain wants to be ready this time and we shall defend our nation at all costs. We believe that Hitler will stop at nothing until all of Europe has become part of the Third Reich. He may try to invade the British Isles."

"That would be madness!" I cried.

"Certainly it would be. The Chancellor and his government may talk of peace, but in fact they take no rational steps. But I am not a politician; I only follow orders."

"What are you working on here?" asked Holmes. "Why are we here?"

Fildes leaned his elbows on the table and folded his hands.

"Gentlemen, what I will now tell you must not leave the confines of these walls. It would cause a panic that we cannot afford."

"Surely you know us by reputation," said my friend.

The microbiologist acknowledged this. He gathered the courage to put his cards on the table.

"My team are working on a research microbe called *Bacillus anthracis* and its potential for military use," he said gravely.

"You are playing with anthrax?!" I said, horrified.

The detective looked at me quizzically.

"Watson?"

I had to explain the seriousness of the situation.

"Surely you've heard of anthrax!" I exclaimed. "Primarily, it is a disease afflicting farm animals, especially cattle. It is highly infectious and is transmitted through the alimentary route, via abrasions on the skin or through the respiratory system. But it can also cause severe illness in humans, which is apparently what Dr Fildes is most interested in… Have you heard of the Hippocratic Oath, sir?"

"You are an idealist, Doctor, if you believe that the enemy does not do the same, and on a much larger scale!" Dr Fildes retorted. "Without us, there would be no effective vaccine against anthrax."

"You are only trying to justify your crime!" I said, not letting up.

"Peace, friend," said the detective, who could see that my blood was boiling.

But he did not know the cruelty that this insidious microbe could inflict on the human body. First the affected person starts to breathe faster; his heartbeat weakens and he feels chest pains. A gelatinous substance builds up around the chest wall; the patient coughs up frothy mucus and dies within three days. All while retaining a clear mind and perception of his suffering. I was outraged. If our government was toying with anthrax, I did not want any part of it.

"How far along are you in your research?" Holmes asked Fildes.

"The Royal Air Force is looking for ways to deliver anthrax spores to enemy territory," he said, shrugging. "They could be placed in conventional aerial bombs and dropped on the enemy. But we have not progressed very far from the theoretical level. And after what has just happened..."

"Yes…"

"One of the most deadly anthrax cultures cultivated here disappeared a few days ago."

The scientist bowed his head. He was responsible for the laboratory and its staff and took this breach very personally.

"Are you trying to say it was stolen..."

"In all likelihood, yes," Fildes said reluctantly.

I gulped. Imagine the immense tragedy this terrible substance could wreak in the wrong hands!

Holmes closed his eyes and rubbed his forehead as though he might faint. Then he shuddered. He looked at me sombrely but with determination. He stood up and stared fixedly out the window at the adjacent laboratory.

"But after all, that is why you are here," said Fildes. "Once we realised that a vial with one culture canker was missing, I reported it. All evidence and documentation has already been provided to the Secret Service. My people will cooperate fully. However, I am glad that you are involved too. The graveness of this case cannot be overstated. It is imperative that the culprit be apprehended as soon as possible!"

I did not have to be a forensic genius to put the facts together.

"Do not worry," said the detective, sighing. "I know who did it."

VI

Audrey

Richard had already announced a leave of absence the week before, so nobody had missed him. Although he was one of the scientists who had access to the substance, nobody had connected its disappearance to him. Fildes therefore looked dumbfounded at Holmes's revelation. Nor did the wind that had been knocked out of him return upon learning that the detective had not come to investigate on behalf of the Defence Ministry, meaning he had revealed more than was necessary. Nevertheless he continued to cooperate. In that small room my friend's authority superseded the amateurish failure of the local personnel to guard their potentially lethal research.

Otherwise Fildes gave Holmes's previous assumptions solid contours. Virtually all of them proved correct. Richard Green had joined Porton Down on the recommendation of Professor Marbury, who had praised his knowledge, creativity and innovativeness. This had occurred a few months ago, after a thorough vetting by the Secret Service. Ironically, the fact that Richard had been recommend to the school by the famous detective had been taken into account. He was given access to the best and most modern equipment, where the need for secrecy was paramount. He was not allowed to publish any of his findings without the consent of his superiors or to lecture at professional congresses. In return the government paid him a handsome salary, much more than his scholarship.

But as we now knew, this had been too little for him. The money that we had found in his flat was no doubt a payment for the anthrax that he had taken from the laboratory. So it had not been drugs, as I had feared, but in fact something far worse. All that remained was to find out who Richard had delivered the anthrax to.

Upon closer examination, the detective finally had to admit that the security at Porton Down was not as poor as it might seem. Each group of ten scientists who worked with anthrax samples had to carefully record their progress. Fildes kept extensive records. Before leaving on holiday Green had falsified them to cover his tracks. What's more, his holiday coincided with equipment maintenance, so he knew that nobody would continue the research for at least two days.

But what he had wanted to do next was anybody's guess. Had he planned to return from his holiday and look startled as though nothing had happened? Would he have attempted to frame a colleague? Had he hung himself because he was tormented by guilt?

"Was Mr Green friends with any of his colleagues? Perhaps he said something or someone noticed something suspicious?"

"I will of course investigate," said the scientist. "My sense was that he was a rather introverted man, but I attributed this to the fact that he was new in the team."

"Can I speak to your people myself?"

Fildes paused.

"With all due respect, Mr Holmes, I accepted you and presumed that you were part of an official investigation. Given that your activity is private, although your involvement in the case has shed new light on it, I dare not give you carte blanche."

"I see. Allow me to ask another way..."

While talking with Dr Fildes Holmes had been making notes in a small notebook, which he now leafed through, looking for the name from the scraps of paper that we had found in Green's stove.

"No, the name Pastor or Pastorius means nothing to me," said Fildes shaking his head. "There is no one of that name here, certainly no one with access to the laboratory."

"Could it be someone from the support staff?"

"We can soon find out," Fildes mused and called the lieutenant who was standing in front of the office and ordered him to carry out an investigation in the administration building.

"Do any of the anthrax samples have the marking LZ 129?" the detective continued.

The doctor raised his eyebrows in genuine surprise.

"No, our markings are completely different."

"Does it mean anything to you?"

"I really do not know," he wondered and rubbed his eyes. "Frankly, I am so consternated by what I have just learned that I cannot keep my thoughts together. I would have never suspected Green. Perhaps you are mistaken and his suicide has nothing to do with our facility."

The youth had apparently made a good impression on Fildes and he struggled to grasp the idea of a traitor in his own team. I understood him, because Holmes and I were in the same situation.

"I indeed wish I were wrong, but it is not so. The facts are the facts. It is an old principle that once you have eliminated the impossible, whatever else is left, no matter how improbable, must be the truth."

"You are probably right, everything fits together... How terrible! In this case what they say about not speaking ill of the dead does not seem to apply and I can think only of words that would insult a common lab rat. After all, the safety of all England is at stake!"

We could offer no objection to the scientist's impassioned words. I myself was perplexed by what

Holmes had said. The detective just clucked disapprovingly, closed the notebook and hid it. And as the lieutenant returned empty-handed, we had to move to other clues.

"Please ask the investigators to contact me at this address," the detective said, jotting down the address of our guesthouse on a card and handing it to Fildes. "Our cases are closely related. The Secret Service will not reject the information that I have to offer; perhaps we will be able to assist each other."

I felt broken as we drove away from Porton Down. In addition to having uncovered Richard's human failures, I was haunted by the task that the scientists had before them. The cattle that now grazed peacefully on the green meadows were soon to become living sacrifices to science. If the scientists succeeded in their research, the world would become a more dangerous place to live in.

Holmes was silent during the whole ride back to London. Instead of returning to the guesthouse Holmes drove back to Mr Green's flat. Although he said it was unlikely we would find anything else, he did not know a different starting point from which we might get to Richard's mistress.

But as we once again climbed the stairs to his flat, we found the door ajar.

"I am certain I locked it," said Holmes, stopping at the edge of the stairs and motioning me to be silent.

We heard a rustling inside.

"What if it's the girl?" I whispered. "Or the landlady?"

"Perhaps," he said quietly. "But given what Richard was involved in, caution is advisable. It could also be the recipient of his deadly shipment."

The idea of a confrontation with a mysterious villain drove the blood to my head. I wished to confront the individual who had led Richard to betray his homeland and to uncover his motive!

"Are you carrying your gun?" the detective asked.

I was not. It was in a compartment under the steering wheel of our car. My instincts in recent days had been numbed not only by age but also the rush of events. But it was no time to retreat, as revealed by the creaking of the stairs. It was a miracle that we had not called attention to ourselves already.

Holmes nodded and strode in with me at his heels. He flung open the door and collided with a tall, slim girl, whose back had been turned to us. He hesitated and tried to grab her arm, but she was ahead of him. I saw a flood of blonde hair under a cap fitted neatly to the side, and then my vision blurred. As soon as the girl detected movement behind her, she whipped around, grabbed the detective's arm, and locked him to her chest with a forearm pressed against his neck in a half nelson.

My friend gasped for breath, but he still possessed the strength of a younger man. He rammed his elbow into the girl's stomach and broke free.

They stood face to face, gasping for breath.

It was obviously the girl from the photograph. But the flat, monochrome world of photography did not capture the young lady's angelic beauty. A small pale face dominated by large, blue-grey eyes and ravishing locks of golden blonde hair. She wore a grey suit and matching hat, whose brim matched her cherry-red lips and high heels. She had the look of a wealthy, upper-class lady. If such a girl returned Richard's love, it was no wonder he was reluctant to bring her to the poor farm of his parents. And that he was trying to make money...

"You are too well dressed to be criminals and too old to be rapists," she said, looking at us quizzically. "Who are you and why have you broken in here?"

The detective showed her the keys in his hand.

"As you can see, we had no intention of breaking in. On the contrary, we are handling the affairs of Mr Green."

"Are you Richard's friends? Are you the ones who made this mess?"

She frowned. And rightfully so. Everywhere there were wind-blown ashes, on the table, the kitchen and on the floor.

"Oh, yes," said Holmes. "But I am afraid that we have more to explain. Perhaps you should sit down."

The girl reluctantly took a seat.

"What's happening? Who are you?"

When we introduced ourselves the girl's eyes lit up.

"But of course, I should have recognised you! Richard talked about you often. He liked to boast of his friendship with the world-famous detective!"

A few days ago this would have given Holmes immense pleasure, but now the young lady's innocent exclamation left a bitter taste. Our cool response immediately made her pause.

"Where is Richard?" she asked with sudden concern. "I have been coming here for a few days and waiting for his return... Why has he not called me? Please tell me where he is."

"What is your name, child?" I asked, sitting down next to her.

"Audrey."

"Richard is dead," the detective said bluntly. He was eyeing her closely.

She looked startled and squeezed my hand until she almost crushed my fingers. Her eyes widened and great tears streamed down her cheeks.

"When did you last see him?" the detective asked, without giving her time to absorb the information. "Did you know where he was the last couple of days?"

"About a week ago," she sobbed.

"And then?"

"We had an argument..." she admitted. "He packed a few things and told me he was going home for a while."

I could feel her trembling. I was afraid she might faint because she slid slightly, but eventually recovered. She took a lace handkerchief out of her purse and wiped her eyes.

"Our relationship was not easy..."

"Really?" I wondered. "He spoke of you as his great love; he wanted to introduce you to his parents!"

"Love was not the problem," she smiled through her tears. "But Richard could not overcome a sense of inferiority that he had in his head. It bothered him that I come from a wealthy family while he is a poor student. He always felt as though he had something to prove."

The detective grunted. But what Audrey said certainly clarified why the humble young man could have begun to lust after money. He saw in it the possibility of securing an appropriate position for his beloved. He loved her so much that it blinded him and led him astray.

"He was so paranoid that he refused even to introduce me to his friends," she continued. "I know that he never talked about me much. It was only recently that I finally convinced him to take me to his parents this summer. It was such an ordeal! Luckily he got a good job and was earning some money..."

"Then why did you fight?"

"He suddenly became nervous, seemed not to listen when I spoke to him. And he would not tell me why. And there was always someone calling him on the telephone. I thought he might have a mistress, but then I was present at one of those calls. I heard a male voice with an accent."

"What were they talking about?"

"I do not know, I did not understand. And Richard quickly ended the call. He was not happy that I had heard it... He was shouting at him, telling him to never call again."

Then she broke into sobs.

"Did he talk to you about his new job?"

"No," she said, wiping the tears from her face. "I only know that it was in a laboratory outside the city. He spent weekdays there and returned to London at the weekend. He held this flat so that we would have a place to be together."

"You are describing a man whom I do not recognise," the detective sighed. "But I am not surprised. We have a reasonable suspicion that Richard was no saint. I cannot tell you the details, but you must know that he was involved in subversive activity."

"No!" she exclaimed. "I would never let something like that happen! I would not jeopardise my family's position to risk being associated with what you are suggesting!"

"Forgive us, we did not want to upset you," I said.

Holmes might be angry at Green, but the girl did not deserve this treatment. I flashed him a look to that effect, but he only raised his eyebrows.

"Miss, I will not apologise for my brusque manner. A young life has been wasted. Years of trust trampled upon. Our homeland betrayed."

"You are mistaken, Richard had nothing to do with it!" she cried indignantly. "Now, Mr Holmes, please leave. I need to be alone. I want to mourn for my love."

"Certainly," he said, escorting her to the door. "We will go. May I have your address? Richard's parents would be happy to get in touch with you. You are all they have left of Richard. You might find solace together."

"Yes, of course," she said more gently, and wrote her London address on a napkin. "If I can help with anything, please contact me. I will be in the city until the end of the week; then I will go to my parents in the country."

"Thank you," said Holmes, placing the napkin in his pocket.

Audrey shook our hands and we said our goodbyes. She took a last look at the flat and then ran down the stairs.

"Poor soul," I said as the sound of her footsteps receded.

I wanted to return to the flat, but the detective grabbed my arm and dragged it.

"Quick, Watson, we must hurry," he commanded, and ran downstairs.

I slammed the door of the flat shut and hurried as fast as I could after him.

"Did you forget something?" I asked.

I caught up to him on the pavement in front of the house, where he suddenly stopped.

In the distance I saw Audrey's shining mane of hair under her cap. She leapt into the driver's seat of a luxury convertible that was parked at the end of the street near a red letterbox and then sped off. Holmes, however, was not looking at her, but on the opposite side of the street, where to my surprise Steiner was sitting in his car.

The detective nodded to him, and the Major sped off after Audrey.

"Where did Steiner come from?" I said amazed.

"He was waiting here the whole time, you just did not notice him," he said dryly.

"And why is he following Audrey?"

He gazed at the horizon of the quiet street in the afternoon light, its budding trees waving gently in the breeze.

"Because I do not believe a word of what she says," he said through clenched teeth.

VII

The Third Floor

I did not understand.

"How can you slander an innocent child?" I cried angrily. "She tried to help us as much as she could! We could barely expect her to be more forthcoming after such a shock!"

"She gave us many motives," he admitted. "Did it not strike you as suspicious?"

"Just that you were too rough with her!"

"Your emotions have once again gotten the better of you, my dear doctor," he said. "In this you are unteachable. But repeat offenders do not change their behaviour, so why should you."

He patted me on the shoulder. The interrogation of Richard's fiancée had suggested something to him that so far eluded me, as always. I was eager to discover what it was.

"First and foremost, I believe that she knew about Richard's suicide, and that what we have just witnessed was simply amateur theatricals," he declared.

"What utter nonsense!" I cried. "How dare you?"

"Did you not notice that she failed to inquire about how Richard died? When? Where? If it was due to an accident or a crime? She had no reason to assume he was suicidal."

I paused for a moment to think and had to admit that he was right. It was indeed strange that she had not asked these questions, but in that turbulent atmosphere it had not occurred to me. But perhaps neither had it occurred to her, and when it all sank in she would attempt to find out. Perhaps she was simply overwhelmed by the news of her lover's death and the details of how it happened were secondary. Holmes listened patiently to my arguments, but was not convinced.

"No, it is human nature upon receiving such news to immediately ask how. The only way she could forget is if she already knew the cause of death and was trying too hard to express emotions in front of us."

I still objected to his accusations against the poor girl.

"I do not blame you, my friend," he said soothingly. "Were I not looking for clues perhaps it would escape me too..."

"Don't keep me in suspense man!"

"We owe it to Major Steiner and Constable Crusher," he explained.

He fumbled in his pockets and again lit his pipe. I had long ago stopped trying to dissuade him from this unhealthy habit.

"Steiner gave me a message from Crusher this morning. After our departure, someone called the Fulworth police station to inquire about Richard. Our dear Crusher was not bashful and told the caller everything about Richard's death, assuming he was talking with a journalist. But it was not a journalist. According to Crusher the voice on the other end was that of a young woman."

"But it could be anyone," I said. "Maybe those people that Audrey said were calling Richard. They could have ascertained that he had fled home."

"Except she claims she heard a male voice. No, there are too many coincidences, and as you know, I do not believe in coincidence. In our case there is so far only one young woman, and until another appears, I am interested in this one."

As always, he finally convinced me that he was correct. I was aware of my weakness, always seeing only the good in women and suffering from a kind of blindness in their presence.

"She did not even take the photograph of them together that was in the bedroom," I pointed out.

"Despite the fact that she searched the flat prior to our arrival," said Holmes. "I remember the condition it was in when we left, and many things were different. Also the empty shelves at the stove were gone. Undoubtedly she knew about the bag with the money. When she learned that Richard died, she came to get it."

This finally had me convinced.

"Lucky that the constable warned you!"

"That's why I told Steiner to rent a second car and watch the flat since morning," said the detective, blowing a puff of smoke into the air. "We'll see what he comes back with."

The good Major returned long after dinner with plenty of interesting news and observations. He had followed Audrey home, to an address that matched the one that she had given Holmes. It was a two-story villa in a prominent area on the outskirts of London. Audrey apparently lived there without her parents, only with her younger brother and servants, who were led by an elderly housekeeper of exotic appearance.

Our suspicions were confirmed by the fact that Audrey returned to the flat later in the evening. She first circled the block a few times to make sure we were gone, then disappeared within for about an hour. But she left empty-handed. Nor could she have found what she was looking for, as the bag full of money was now safely stored in a bank vault. Disappointed she went home, where she remained for the rest of the night.

But the diligent Steiner did not end his investigation there. He stopped his car in front of the house and feigned mechanical trouble in order to draw out the groundskeeper, from whom he gained valuable insight into the girl's family. The man confirmed that the young lady's parents lived on their country estate year round and hardly ever came into the city. Their wealth, according to him, came from owning pharmaceutical companies and factories.

"Fascinating," said Holmes. "Especially the last part."

I too was intrigued to learn about the business activities of Audrey's family. Their name was not unknown in the medical profession and I understood the direction that the detective's thoughts were taking. There was a clear motive here. The stolen anthrax culture could be a priceless commercial treasure, mainly thanks to the sale of the antidote.

"This would mean that Audrey not only knew more about Richard's plans than she is telling us, but that she may be directly involved in the crime leading to his death," I said. "We must confront her again!"

"You are right, Watson," he said. "But we do not have to engage her in a frontal attack. Audrey is a sly fox; we cannot assume that she will capitulate if we strike at her merely with conjecture, but without evidence. The facts and nothing but the facts! If we are right in suspecting that she and her family are behind everything, we must act cautiously. Fortunately, we have the bait..."

"The satchel with the money?"

"Exactly," he said, snapping his fingers. "Now the question is, how best to set the trap?"

***

Our visit to Audrey's villa was unexpected, but certainly welcome. At least, so we surmised from the expression on our hostess's face when we appeared the next day at the gate. We were shown into the spacious drawing room by a liveried butler and settled into luxurious dark leather armchairs.

"I am so glad to meet you," said Audrey to Richard's parents, whom we had brought with us for the visit. "I had no idea that you would consider making a trip to London. Mr Holmes is so very kind to have brought us together. Richard would certainly be happy."

Richard's parents, who for the purposes of our ruse were played by Major Steiner in a false beard and his plump wife, portrayed their roles brilliantly. Were they theatre actors I would have applauded their performance. The first half hour of our meeting was again a vale of tears. If Audrey was indeed playing a part, she was a truly gifted actress. For a long time she spoke about Richard, taking a lively interest in his childhood and his life before his studies.

"If only I knew what it would lead to!" Mrs Steiner cried.

"I will do anything to help Mr Holmes find out what Richard was involved in," said Audrey hugging her. "Since yesterday I can think of nothing else!"

"Have you recalled anything that might help us find the man who telephoned?"

"Since you mention it, yes, though I did not want to discuss this sensitive topic in front of the Greens," said the girl, lowering her eyes and staring at the damp handkerchief in her hands. "As I said, the man had an accent. And the more I think about it, the more I am convinced that he was Italian."

"Italian?"

"Yes, I think the man was Italian," she said.

"Hmm, I wonder..." said the detective.

Then he clutched his head. "Indeed, how did it not occur to me earlier?"

"What happened?"

"Audrey, do you have an atlas of Europe?" Holmes asked.

"Yes, certainly, upstairs in the study," she said blinking, and called the butler. "Jeeves, is Mrs T here? She will know exactly where everything is – she is my housekeeper of many years," she added by way of explanation to us.

"She is running errands in town, Miss," said the footman shaking his head.

"Then ask Leonard to come here," said Audrey, whereupon a boy of about ten was called into the drawing room.

He immediately caught my attention. I do not usually care much for small children – they are noisy, unruly, clumsy and generally bothersome – but this one was different. Despite his youth he had an extremely clever and perceptive appearance, and the movements of his body were almost adult-like, free of that childish awkwardness and lack of coordination. He was dressed in a navy blue school uniform and red cap with visor, from beneath which protruded jet-black hair, almost the same colour as his lively eyes.

"Leonard, come greet our guests," Audrey called. "Allow me to introduce you to my brother. Will you take Mr Holmes upstairs and show him to the library; he needs to find something. Be a good fellow."

The boy nodded and led the detective away by the hand. It was touching to watch a man in the twilight of his life walking hand in hand with a small boy before whom the world's magic and secrets were just being uncovered.

"Interesting how different you are," I said, pointing out the boy's dark hair and facial structure, which was far wider than that of the ethereal Audrey.

"I resemble mother and Leonard is more like father," she said automatically, as though she were accustomed to answering the same question often.

They were gone for about twenty minutes, during which time the conversation with the Greens gradually began to stagnate. When Holmes and Leonard finally returned, the detective was carrying the requested book.

"It seems like you really hit the nail on the head," my friend cried from the stairs, waving the atlas. "Obviously, we must take a trip to Italy!"

"I am so glad!" Audrey smiled, who, unlike me, did not show surprise.

"I did not yet tell you that we found some destroyed notes in Richard's flat. I really thought they could not be deciphered, but now I think I have," said Holmes, and he sat next to the girl and opened the atlas on his lap.

"The ashes..." her eyes widened with recognition.

"Yes, I was able to make out the word Pastor or Pastorius, it's hard to tell exactly," he explained, leafing through the maps. "And then two days spent scouring around Richard for someone of that name, but in vain. After all, it is not the name of a man, but of a city! Look!"

He pointed in the atlas at the Italian city of Pastoria.

Audrey stared, and I could see that her skill as an actress was being put to the test. She blinked furiously. I was sure that she had heard the name.

"That's a good clue," she said slowly. "Did you find anything else in the ashes?"

"The marking LZ 129, but that is still a mystery to me," said the detective. "But do not worry, I will figure it out sooner or later."

He returned the heavy book to Leonard. "You can put it away, boy."

"I do not doubt you, sir," said Audrey. "You continue to prove that your powers of deduction have not dimmed with age."

She adjusted her hair and pondered for a moment.

"I have the utmost conviction in your logic," she finally said. "I too want to know what drove Richard into this hopeless situation. If I may, I would like to finance your trip to Pastoria. It is the least I can do."

Once again her immediate offer to help confused me. Holmes had convinced me that the girl was at the centre of the case, so why was she so willing to cooperate?

Mrs Steiner felt that it would be a good idea to do something and sniffed loudly.

"That is most generous of you," said Holmes, stroking Audrey's face with a fatherly gesture. "For a retired detective such a trip is expensive. But I think it will not be necessary. The Greens are paying the expense of the investigation."

"Please do not accept anything from them!" she said. "They cannot afford it!"

The detective smiled innocently.

"Mr Green secured his parents before his death," said Holmes, laying his trap. "His legacy includes a substantial monetary pay-out. Perhaps his after-school job was much more lucrative than it seemed. And it will only be right if part of that money is used to uncover the reason for his death."

Audrey returned the chequebook that she had meanwhile taken out of her desk.

"Very well, as you think best," she said, biting her lower lip slightly. "Then I will wish you good luck. And please do keep me informed."

"I promise that I will always remember you," the detective said.

We went into the vestibule, where Audrey bade a last emotional farewell to the supposed parents of her beloved, and pledged that if in the future they needed anything they must not hesitate to turn to her. Little Leonard also came to say goodbye. I had never seen such a peaceful and orderly child! I commended his sister on his upbringing.

"He is so quiet!" I said.

"He is just shy," said his sister, patting him on the head. "I am sure it will pass."

"I wish all children were like him," I said.

"In a perfect world they will be," she replied. "And perfection is the future to which we are headed!"

"An interesting idea," said Holmes. "Although I would argue that how one defines perfection may vary greatly. It is imperative that this contradiction not lead to conflict."

Mrs Steiner again broke the awkward silence. The Major was helping her into her coat, but it turned out that it was too small.

"It is not mine, this must be yours," she said looking at the coat and handing it back to Audrey. "Excuse me, such a beautiful piece. Is it a Steilmann?"

The girl's eyes widened.

"I do not know that salon," she said, clearing her throat. "The coat is from Piccadilly."

Mrs Steiner nodded and put on the right coat, which at first glance really was similar in colour and length to Audrey's. A few moments later we stepped out the door.

"Do not walk too quickly," the detective said to our group as we headed up the path to the car.

He shuffled slowly, as though he were a decade older, delaying our departure as long as he could. He lit his pipe, straightened his back, studied the flowers and shrubs in the garden, listened to the birds...

"What is this all about, Holmes?" I whispered. "Will we really go to Italy?"

"I shall tell you in the car," he said, slowly hobbling around.

But he kept his promise.

"A beautiful building is it not?" he said, waving at Audrey's villa as Steiner started the car. "A marvellous example of modern architecture that respects tradition and fits perfectly into the environment."

"I would say that you were waiting for me to notice something specific," I commented.

"Indubitably."

I glanced over my shoulder to get another look at the house, which disappeared behind the rear window. There seemed nothing suspicious about it.

"I shall not keep you in suspense," said Holmes, chuckling. "The construction of the façade and interior layout that I have had the chance to briefly explore at first glance appears to be two-storey. Its residents give this semblance utmost support, turning attention away from it as they can. But when you look more closely, you will notice that there is a third floor hidden under the roof, though I found no stairway or other access to it."

"That's why you stayed in the bathroom so long," I said.

I had feared that his prostate was bothering him, an ailment that had already troubled the detective in the past. But he had simply taken advantage of the fact that nobody was watching him to do some reconnaissance work.

"Perhaps it's just a common attic," I suggested.

"No, it is too hidden and inaccessible."

The secret floor of Audrey's house had sparked his curiosity.

"I would like to know what secrets it hides!"

VIII

Old Hatred Never Dies

I tried for a long time to talk Holmes out of this nocturnal expedition. I thought that the years of creeping into the houses of suspects and dangerous villains were already long behind us. We had ventured to engage in similar acrobatics for the past fifteen years, and I was convinced that our physical condition, no matter how well maintained, was no longer up to the task.

"Send Steiner," I said. "He has proven himself adept at detective work."

"Steiner is a clever man and a good soldier, but that is not enough for the job," he said dismissively. "What Audrey is hiding upstairs is crucial to our case."

I realised that Holmes had stopped using the conditional when discussing the girl's involvement in the case. Though he explained that her support for the Pastoria expedition was surely just a diversionary tactic, I still hesitated to condemn her out of hand.

"Does it not seem to you a stretch that Audrey and her family would organise the theft of a closely guarded government programme for their own pharmaceutical research? That would mean that she met Richard with this goal in mind. But how did she learn about it in the first place?"

"I have a theory that explains it. If we find what I really think upstairs, I will be happy to explain it to you. You will be surprised by how blind you were!"

"We are over eighty years old," I pointed out. "How are you going to get there? Do you remember when you wanted to climb the ladder to the loft where that ferret was hiding? How did that go? And as far as I remember there are no trees next to the house and the façade is too smooth to be scaled."

"You do not have to remind me of my age, Watson, I realise it every morning," he snapped.

"Besides, I am no Presbury," he added, in reference to our earlier adventure with the Creeping Man, who had attempted to halt the aging process using the serum of a Langur monkey.

"And if as you say the house hides important secrets it will certainly be well guarded," I said. "Even if we enter at night, it will hardly be freely accessible."

"This is the lesser of our two immediate problems," he said. "In the back of the garden I saw a dog kennel. I assume that at night the garden is guarded by dogs. I do not expect any guards within. Audrey wants to preserve the appearance of normality and does not want to attract attention. Besides herself and her brother, only the housekeeper and butler live in the house. She relies on secrecy, which is why I think we shall not encounter any bodyguards."

"And if you are wrong?"

"If I am wrong, you shall have your revolver at the ready. Please do try not to forget it this time."

And so that night we found ourselves back at the luxurious villa. Holmes had in the meantime made several telephone calls and given Steiner instructions in case we did not return before morning. The villa was bathed in moonlight and all was still. Steiner even dropped us off a few blocks further away so that we would not be betrayed by the rumbling of the car's motor. The only thing we now heard was the rustling of the package in my pocket.

We were already out of breath when we arrived at the main gate.

A dark growl behind the fence told us that the dogs had already registered our visit. I placed my glasses on my forehead and discerned in the darkness two massive Dobermans with shiny coats. They bared their teeth at us and paced ominously closer.

I opened my package and threw two lean chops over the fence. The dogs hesitated, sniffed the meat, but did not touch it. My plan to stun them was a failure. The chops were infused with a tranquiliser agent that would stun even a lion. But these animals were too well trained to trust food from strangers. On the contrary, it caused them to growl louder. I was afraid that at any moment they would start barking.

"We have to go to Plan B," Holmes sighed.

He moved back and I pulled on my gloves and went along the fence. The dogs followed me, not letting me out of their sight. While I served as a diversion, I watched Holmes out of the corner of my eye.

He hid behind a pillar at the gate where the Dobermans could not see him. He wrapped his scarf around his face, like a burglar, until only his eyes peeped out. Then he took from his bag a pile of rags, which he wrapped around his palms. Thus prepared he climbed the wall, and holding onto the post, clawed over the fence and into the garden.

The dogs immediately lost interest in me and shot like arrows right at Holmes. He had barely had time to stagger up and they fell upon him. It was an awful sight. Like rampaging wild animals they gathered a full head of steam and knocked him to the ground with the weight of their muscular bodies, sinking their teeth into his outstretched hands. I stared with horror at the writhing tangle of bodies, fearing that Holmes's plan had failed, and grabbed the gun before it was too late and the Dobermans tore my friend limb from limb.

But in the end I did not have to pull the trigger. In tearing at the pieces of rags the dogs had inhaled the ether in which they had been soaked, and now slumped about drowsily, until they tumbled to the ground in a motionless heap. I clambered as quickly as I could over the fence and joined the detective in the garden. He was still lying on the ground. There were a few lacerations on his face and his clothes were also torn, but otherwise he was all right. He slowly and carefully lifted himself up.

"I expect Mrs Steiner will scold me about the state of my clothes," he said, examining the holes in his plaid jacket and trousers. "But she will not have to launder them. They will go straight into the trash."

I helped him take off the rags. The dogs would sleep until morning, but they would wake up. The detective had respect for all living things, and had taken care not to overdose them.

"We could have had your chops for dinner," he joked.

We left the dogs and crept towards the next obstacle: the entrance to the villa itself.

At least Holmes acknowledged that I was right about one thing and had given up the idea of penetrating the house by climbing the facade or jumping from a tree. His plan, however, was only slightly less audacious. He intended to enter through the cellar, which meant that we had to locate the entrance to the mysterious third floor from the inside, and creep through the whole villa in order to get there.

The hatch that covered the steps to the basement was secured with a padlock, which the detective expertly picked. Then he shut the hatch again behind us.

We lit torches and looked around. The room was windowless and mostly empty. Pipes snaked over the low ceiling. I was momentarily shocked by the outline of a male figure in front of me, but it was just a mannequin. But not just any mannequin like one would find in a tailor's workshop. It was covered with black leather and in place of limbs it had long wooden spikes and finials. The whole contraption was placed on a rotating platform.

"Audrey continues to amaze me," Holmes murmured. "This is a fighting mannequin, used in Asian martial arts training."

He pushed one of the spikes and it swivelled on its axis.

The cellar contained numerous other such devices. Audrey apparently used it as a private gym, where she trained her body. There were mats, wall bars, a long bench, a punching bag and barbells of various sizes and weights.

"Who would have thought it of that girl?"

"Richard too was a fine athlete; he was obviously impressed," said the detective.

It was now time to head upstairs to the first floor. The stairs from the cellar led to the lobby beneath a much more elegant staircase leading to the next floor. We peered out from the entrance. The sound of the hinges creaking as we carefully opened the door was like a rooster crowing. I prayed it did not have the same effect.

The house was silent.

The detective had guessed correctly that there would be no guards. The residents inadvertently did us a favour by leaving a small lamp in the drawing room lamp lit, either out of carelessness, or because the owners did not like the dark. Its dim light illuminated the hallway. We therefore did not have to use the torches that could give us away and scurried upstairs like mice in the shadows. Holmes did not look around too much; he followed his nose.

"The ground floor has a kitchen, dining room, common areas and rooms for servants. On the first floor there is an office, a library and a nursery," he said, impressing me with his peerless observational talent. He must have made a mental map of the house when he went to the bathroom. "On the second floor are the bedrooms."

I nodded and headed to the second floor, but he stopped me.

"The access to the secret room is not from Audrey's bedroom. The difference in the size of the windows is visible from within and from without. So either the house has unusually thick walls or there is a passage hidden behind the wall."

The study and adjacent library led to a corridor to the left. Therefore Leonard's bedroom and playroom had to be on the right.

"I wonder, has the boy a nanny?" I whispered.

"I did not notice signs of anybody like that," the detective replied. "The boy has outgrown them. Do not worry; I counted the household members carefully."

I trusted his words, and whatever happened over the next hours, the numbers were not something I could blame Holmes for getting wrong.

The study reflected the personality of its owner: meticulous and orderly. A mahogany desk stood against the window, which let in enough moonlight for us to see clearly. The items on the desk were arranged precisely. The writing pad was at right angles with the diary and a box for pens. On the right there was a telephone and on the left a sheaf of papers.

"Only accounts, nothing interesting," said Holmes, going through it quickly.

Facing the chair, back to the door, was a photograph, but not of Green. We did not recognise the people in it, but I assumed they were Audrey's parents.

Holmes was much more interested in the walls, whose thickness the detective disputed. He suspected it was only a fake. Part of the wall was occupied by a bar, while another had a shelf with artefacts from around the world. The girl must have travelled a lot. There were rare carved statuettes of African ivory, Asian masks, traditional amulets of Australian aborigines, objects from Nepal, India and others that I could not place. She also apparently collected figurines of angels; there were dozens of different depictions and different materials – ceramic, crystal, gold, gypsum, and others and others. There was one among them that stood out, not only because it was black as ebony, but because its material was so unusual.

"Better not touch anything here," Holmes said.

I would have listened to him, but my hand was already in motion. And then something odd happened. I touched the figurine, but although it was tiny and should have moved, it instead remained firmly mounted on the shelf.

I called the detective, who examined it closely.

"Thank God for your inquisitiveness," he said, and he grabbed the figurine by its head.

He turned it clockwise, and it moved smoothly, triggering a spring right below it. A hidden mechanism moved the entire wall, which parted like a doorway, revealing a narrow staircase, exactly as Holmes had expected, leading directly to the attic.

We clambered up and found the second study. It was much less lavish than the first; in fact, it was a common attic with a small skylight, but it contained two important items: a radio transmitter and a steel safe.

"There is no longer any doubt," I said.

The detective sat next to the radio and shone his flashlight on it. He carefully transcribed the frequency in his notebook. He looked around, but there were no notes or encryption book anywhere to be seen.

"There was never any doubt," he said absently. "Audrey is an accomplished spy. The contents of that safe will reveal who she is working for."

I had no idea how he intended to open the safe, but as always he had an ace up his sleeve. Indeed, a British firm specialising in the manufacture of safes had once called upon him to test their wares, for he had had no little experience of safe breakers, who thanks to him now dwelt in prisons throughout the Isles. All he needed was a stethoscope, a wire clamp and a piece of string, and half an hour later the wheel of the vault moved, and the door swung open.

But there was one thing he had not expected.

The safe must have been connected to a hidden alarm triggered by this unauthorised opening. The villa rattled with a deafening clanging that could probably be heard in the centre of London. I felt faint.

"Run!" I cried, trying to shout over the alarm and pulling Holmes away.

"I would say it is pointless," he said haughtily. "There is nowhere to go. We cannot run up, and we are unlikely to get out through the house. We are outnumbered after all."

He was right. Beneath the secret staircase a light came on and there was a stomping as someone ran up. The detective looked untroubled and quietly studied the contents of the safe. Over his shoulder I could see vials similar to those that Fildes had shown us at Porton Down, the ones in which anthrax was kept in the laboratory. But the one in the safe was empty. Holmes ignored it and quickly scanned the contents of the files that were stacked there.

Little Leonard stuck his head through the entrance hatch. He was wearing a nightshirt, but otherwise seemed lively, as though he had not been sleeping. And it must have been three o'clock in the morning!

"You should go back to bed," I barked. "This is an adult matter."

He glared at me and somersaulted from the stairs straight toward me. I did not expect this and tried to push him away, but in vain. This child did not behave at all like a child! Though I abhor capital punishment, I attempted to slap him, but he easily dodged me. He leapt behind me, grabbed my arm, twisted it behind his back and threw me violently against the wall with the strength of a grown man.

I rolled over onto my back. Leonard stood straddled over me and clenched his fists. The ten-year-old boy was fighting like a highly trained soldier. I could see in his cold eyes that it would take very little for him to kill me.

The alarm suddenly stopped. Someone downstairs must have turned it off.

Holmes stood up from the safe and put away the files that he had managed to read. He did not venture into a confrontation that he knew was hopeless. It was enough that he had the answers to his questions. I hoped he would have the chance to tell me before we died.

We could hear footsteps on the stairs. Then Audrey's housekeeper, whose acquaintance we had not yet had the pleasure to make, clambered into the room.

"Mrs T? I presume that this uninvited guest will be our dear Mr Holmes."

The voice from the study was that of Audrey.

The housekeeper nodded. She was a few years younger than us, but time had not been kind to her. Her face was like a shrivelled raisin, but in terms of physical condition she was no slouch. Her hair was still jet-black, with a single thread of grey on the left temple. She held a sharp curved machete in one hand and quickly frisked us with the other. She pushed Holmes away from the safe and took my revolver. As she pulled it out of my pocket, she placed the blade of her deadly weapon on my neck. I dared not move an inch.

Then she spit in my face. I do not know why she chose me, when she had scores to settle with Holmes…

As it turned out, the mysterious Mrs T was our old adversary, the Indian assassin Naya. I recognised her immediately. So did the detective, even though the sari had been replaced with European dress. After forty years it was a most unexpected reunion.

She handed the gun to Leonard, who assessed it with an expert's eye. In his tiny hands it looked like a toy. My brain was still struggling to comprehend the contrast between his appearance and behaviour.

Downstairs in the office the telephone rang.

Audrey picked up the receiver and I heard her talking with someone.

"We're fine, Lieutenant, thank you for calling. Code word *cuckoo*. Yes, nothing happened," she chirped sweetly. "I have carelessly triggered the alarm by mistake. I apologise. Goodbye. Certainly I will attend your charity ball... You too, goodnight."

Then she joined us in the attic. When she entered she turned on the light switch and we could finally all see each other clearly.

"The alarm is connected to the local precinct," she said, almost apologetically. "I should not want them to disturb us. I hope you did not hurt the dogs? Tanuja, please go check on them. Leonard has had them since they were puppies."

"I would not hurt an innocent soul," said Holmes with steely composure. "The same cannot be said of you, madam."

"You suspected me from the beginning, did you not?"

Her voice and manner were as calm and casual as his.

"It was about five minutes after our first encounter," he said. "I know that you met Richard prior to his joining Porton Down, so it is unlikely that you planned it beforehand."

"You are right. At first he was just an outstanding chemist whom the Reich had identified for recruitment. That a certain unique opportunity arose was merely good fortune. Evidence of how the gods favour our mission."

My jaw fell when I heard what she said.

"The Reich? What Reich?" I gasped, even though I knew the answer.

"Surely the Third one, Doctor," she said, smiling at my astonishment.

Then she stood at attention and extended her right arm in the air in the Nazi salute.

"*Heil* Hitler!" she cried, her eyes blazing with fire, a fire that had the power to burn the entire world.

IX

Child's Play

Had I not already been lying on the ground I would have keeled over.

"Let me explain it to you, my dear Watson," said Holmes, folding his hands behind his back. "Or would you prefer to do the honours, madam?"

"Not at all; I would be delighted to hear the great detective's interpretation," said Audrey with a giggle.

She sat down on the stool next to the radio and crossed one leg over the other, revealing a slender white calf under her bathrobe. "Because I will never get the chance to read your case," she added ominously, glancing at Naya and her machete.

"As a Nazi spy you seduced Richard and used him to steal the anthrax samples for you," said Holmes. "You plan to start a war, to attack not only Europe but the United States! I know all about your Operation Pastorius."

"You disappoint me, Mr Holmes," she sighed. "I have just old you myself that I serve Germany. The rest you read in the documents in the safe..."

"I already knew that you are a Nazi," Holmes retorted. "And I think you realised I suspected it."

She smiled, genuinely this time.

"Yes, Steilmann... That coat which Mrs Green mistakenly put on. No village grandmother would know the work of the best tailor in all Berlin. I know that I shouldn't wear it here, but it is just so... chic!"

"You have demonstrated great imprudence, my dear" said Holmes. "You are no Mata Hari*. For a supposedly elite agent of the Abwehr** you have allowed yourself to be caught like a rank amateur."

"The important thing is results, Holmes," she said. "I have fulfilled my task. As soon as you started sniffing around me, I sent the shipment to safety."

"I see..." he turned to the safe and pointed to the empty vials. "It was not Richard's idea to keep you a secret from his family and friends, but yours! Once he had served his purpose, you got rid of him, isn't that so?"

"You are gravely mistaken," she said. "But indeed I underestimated him. When I met him, he was a poor village boy, whose intellect was readily for sale. He so wanted to achieve something. Sex and money were all that interested him..."

"But then you hit a roadblock," said Holmes. "Richard allowed himself to be persuaded to steal the anthrax, but he did not know that he was betraying his country."

"The fool really believed that it would help my family's business," she said. "All these great minds, these chemists, physicists and Nobel laureates, are so naive in real life... He thought he could prove to my father that he was worthy of me. For half a year I patiently directed his thoughts and worldview; I thought that he was ready. I gave him everything a young man could want!"

"But you did not take into account his conscience," I said.

"When he discovered that he had fallen in love with and delivered anthrax to a Nazi spy, he panicked and fled," Holmes said. "He did not believe in the Third Reich, but could not bring himself to give you up to the authorities. He was so ashamed of his actions that he chose to escape from life."

After the truth had been revealed there was silence in the attic.

Leonard and Tanuja, who I still thought of as Naya, looked at each other curiously. They were waiting for an order from their mistress. I doubted that the boy was actually Audrey's brother. From everything I had heard about German doctors, he might have been the result of their experiments in human breeding.

"Gentlemen, I was truly sorry about Richard's death," Audrey said, helping me to my feet. "Just as I will be sorry about yours. But there is no place in this world for those who do not believe in our worldview or try to prevent it from coming about."

I stood proudly beside Holmes, waiting for the Hindu or for Leonard to carry out the execution. Neither of us feared death.

Audrey, however, had no intention of killing us now.

"Gentlemen, before we say goodbye forever, I have a proposition for you," she said. "I want my money back."

A faint smile ran across Holmes's face. That's why he was so calm the whole time! He knew that she would not touch a hair on our heads until she had the Nazi money back.

"Is the Chancellor broke?" he asked mockingly.

"The world is heading into an expensive war," she said. "But the truth is that the Chancellor will not miss the money. I am not a charity. I shall find a better use for it."

So it was simple greed then. Greed that would determine the fate of millions.

"Why should I help you obtain it?"

"I realise that it makes little sense to threaten two old men with the prospect of death," she said. "At this point most people would be surprised to learn that you are actually alive. But I presume you would not want me to go to Fulworth to get the money. I think that one tragedy in the family is enough."

Holmes's decoy had turned against us. We could not put the Greens in jeopardy.

"Very well," said Holmes, lowering his shoulders in defeat. "You will get your money."

"Excellent, we shall go at once," said Audrey.

"No need. The money is not in Fulworth. We found it in Richard's flat and placed it in a safety deposit box at the bank of Sewell and Barnaby."

"So much the better, unless you are lying," she said, looking at him suspiciously.

"I took it there myself," I said.

"Sewell and Barnaby have a night shift," she said, looking at her watch. It was three-thirty. "We shall do it this way. As Mr Holmes might be tempted to try something on the way, he shall remain here as our hostage. Watson shall go to retrieve the money and Leonard shall go with him. The doctor shall take the money from the safe deposit box and deliver it here."

I was not pleased to be considered so harmless that a child could guard me, and was even more alarmed to be separated from Holmes. I made this clear.

"It will be fine," said the detective, winking at me. "Follow her instructions and bring the money."

"If you cooperate, you have my word that nothing will happen to the Greens," said Audrey. "Richard's suicide will remain unresolved and I will guarantee you a quick death."

I would not call it a happy ending, but the detective looked pleased. The girl motioned for us to sit on the stool, back to back, and Leonard tightly bound us together with rope. He did not even leave our legs loose.

"You must wait here while we prepare the car," she said, meanwhile emptying the safe of its contents, which she tossed on a pile in the middle of the room. "When the doctor returns, you will burn together with the house and all the evidence."

When the safe was empty she picked up a book and threw it into my lap.

"You can read meanwhile," she said.

I looked at the cover of the book. It was *Mein Kampf*. I had had it in my hands once before and was in no mood to read that tirade of bile and hatred.

"A shame about the house," said Holmes when the trio of villains had left. He leaned against my back and rested, gathering his strength.

For a few minutes I strained my ears to hear if it was a trap and if they were not perchance listening to us. I waited for the detective to begin struggling with the handcuffs. But he did not attempt an escape.

"How can you be so calm?" I said. "Our lives no longer matter, but the anthrax could inflict enormous damage!"

"I am aware of that, but we can only do what we are able," he said. "At the moment our options are limited. It is ridiculous that we were disarmed by a young lady, a seventy-year-old woman and a child of ten, but none of them is of the ordinary variety. Certainly not the boy! In the safe I found formulas for strengthening the body and mind. The gym in the basement is his training room."

"I agree, but that is hardly important right now..."

"On the contrary," Holmes retorted. "As the child is now our jailer, I believe it is crucial to know your enemy. Listen to me, Watson: do not attempt a daring escape. The boy is a formidable opponent!"

I wondered at his fatalism, but we did not have time to discuss it further, as the boy was now returning. He was dressed in a miniature driver's uniform and leather gloves, resembling a dwarf more than a child. He held the revolver which he had confiscated from me and pointed it at me.

He untied me from Holmes and shoved me down the stairs to the study.

The lights were on in the house and there was a lot of commotion. Audrey and Tanuja had changed out of their nightgowns and had whatever they needed from the house before its destruction. A valet who was helping them greeted me politely, but otherwise seemed not the least bit nonplussed by the fact that his employer was holding the famous detective hostage in the attic.

"Leonard, you have until dawn," Audrey told the boy. "Then we have to go. We will not wait. You have your instructions, including permission to eliminate the doctor if he tries something. Now move!"

The boy took me in front of the house where he waited in the driveway and parked a lorry. The fact that they had been able to arrange everything in such a brief time showed that they were prepared for any situation.

He sat me in the passenger seat and fastened the seatbelt. He loosened the ropes on my feet just enough for me to walk, but did not release my hands at all.

"Will it not be strange to enter the bank in handcuffs?"

"Do not worry, *Herr Doktor*," he said in a high-pitched, German-accented voice. It was the first time he had spoken. No wonder he had not said a word before; it would have immediately disclosed his origins.

We drove into the dark streets. It was almost an hour until dawn. Plenty of time to reach the bank and return with the money.

The boy was driving expertly, even though his head was barely visible above the big steering wheel. The pedals were attached to a sort of extension that would allow him to comfortably reach them with his short legs. From the outside, it must have appeared as though the car was driving itself. He put the revolver on the seat between his legs, in case I should attempt to overpower him. But I had no such intention, for I had decided to listen to Holmes's instructions and cooperate. I hoped that he knew what he was doing. Perhaps he had a plan to gain control of the house during Leonard's absence.

As we neared the bank, instead of slowing down Leonard accelerated. We raced through populated areas, and around us were tall buildings, whose residents were still asleep. The lorry bumped and jostled as it sped over the cobblestone streets. I did not understand why we are driving so fast until I noticed in the rear-view mirror the headlights of a car that was matching our speed.

"Somebody's following us?"

"You play a dangerous game," the boy cried.

He must have thought that the driver of the car was familiar to me. Had Holmes prepared an ambush with Steiner? But no, I had heard the detective order him to wait for us in the guesthouse. The alarm should have been triggered only if we did not return in the morning.

Our lorry negotiated several sharp turns. Leonard tried to shake the pursuer between the houses, but the other driver was no amateur. As he neared, I recognised an Aston Martin that certainly did not belong to anyone I knew.

"Grab the wheel and hold it steady," Leonard commanded and took the gun. "If you turn it, we both die."

I grabbed the steering wheel with both hands and tried not to crash into the cars parked along the road. I do not know what I would do if another car or a pedestrian were to cross our path from one of the side streets.

The boy released the pedals, turned and jumped on the seat with his legs braced on the back of the headrest and began to fire at the pursuer. The car swerved to avoid the bullets. Judging by the sound of breaking glass, Leonard had managed to hit it. The car skidded, the brakes squealed and it came to a stop. Leonard sank back on the seat next to me and replaced his feet on the pedals.

He laughed childishly, as though he had found a coveted gift under the Christmas tree or was playing a delightful game.

But this was the game of life.

Then the lights in the rear-view mirror again shone bright, levelled with the road and continued the pursuit. The driver had lost a few precious seconds, but his car was faster than our lorry and was almost immediately upon us.

Leonard cursed.

The car matched our speed and for a moment both vehicles were side by side. Now I could see the driver.

It was not Steiner, but a handsome, middle-aged man in an elegant suit, whose handkerchief matched his tie. He was clean-shaven with short, neatly combed hair, which despite the wild ride did not seem disturbed in the least. For a brief moment he looked me directly in the eye and winked.

"Hold on," he called through the whistling air.

Before my ten-year-old kidnapper knew what was happening, the man swerved sharply and rammed us from the side at speed. The metal of both vehicles creaked and sparks flew. The lorry barely stayed on the road, but it continued on. I was lucky that the little Nazi had fired all the bullets, because now he would have used the weapon against me. But he had been ordered to either bring me back with the money or not at all.

The man in the Aston Martin repeated the manoeuvre twice more. On the third attempt Leonard could no longer keep the lorry under control and struck a lamppost. The lorry spun around and rolled over on the passenger side where I was sitting. My head was just inches from the pavement as the car slid across the road. The little driver screamed angrily and held like a tick to the wheel. Then we crashed into something and abruptly stopped. The impact threw my head against the dashboard and shattered the windshield. Leonard let go of the steering wheel and fell right next to me.

We were both lying on the ground. The boy did not move. I felt a trickle of blood running down my neck, but I could not tell whether it was mine.

The Aston Martin pulled over nearby. The driver slammed the door and walked towards us. From my point of view on the ground all I could see were expensive loafers with a perforated toe.

"Are you all right?" the man asked, leaning over me.

"Define all right," I croaked.

"You are alive," he said dryly. "That is enough."

His stoicism reminded me of Holmes as a young man.

"Who are you?"

He introduced himself and handed me his card. The logo in the top left corner said Universal Exports.

* Mata Hari was a Dutch oriental dancer, who during the First World War became an agent of Germany and France. She presented a fictional life story, performed in circuses, posed for painters and was a renowned dancer of exotic dances. She was also known as a courtesan and mistress of many notables.

** The German secret service.

X

On His Majesty's Secret Service

I did not know much about Universal Exports, except that it was a shell company of His Majesty's Secret Service. I knew about its existence only through my collaboration with Sherlock Holmes, whose brother Mycroft was once its long-time director. In his honour, all future directors encrypted their civil service names with the first letter of his first name, "M".

Naturally, I shall not reveal here the name of the agent who knocked over Leonard's lorry. Although I suspect it was merely a code name, I do not want to risk exposing government secrets. So I shall call him James. Within the organisation of which he was a part he had attained to the rank of captain.

"How did you find me? Who sent you?" I groaned.

My body had suffered more than its fair share of trials and tribulations over the past few hours. It was no easy task to stand up.

With James's help, however, I succeeded in getting to my feet. Together we pulled the unconscious Leonard out of the lorry. His small body was surprisingly heavy. He was solid as a rock, all muscle.

"I am investigating a security breach at Porton Down and you and your friend have been at the focus since Dr Fildes filed a report about your visit," the agent explained. "This afternoon I got a call from my commanding officer, who said that Mr Holmes had informed him of his suspicions regarding a certain young lady and his intention to verify them. I was sent to monitor the situation."

"Holmes was right," I confirmed, and told him everything that had happened that night. "The lady is a German spy and has stolen anthrax!"

"Where is the anthrax now? Did you find it?"

"She moved it before we broke into her house."

James cursed and lit a cigarette, seemingly untroubled by the fact that the tank of the lorry against which he was leaning was leaking petrol onto the road.

"We have been watching the villa since late afternoon and nobody left or came. They must have moved it before, right after your afternoon visit. I would have helped you before, but we had orders not to interfere. We needed the lady to incriminate herself. Mr Holmes believed that he could scare her and that she would run into our arms with the anthrax in her hands."

"Alas, we ran into her arms."

James nodded.

"As soon as I saw you being led away in handcuffs by that elf it was clear that something was wrong. My colleagues remained on patrol and I set off in pursuit of the lorry."

"We must go back to Holmes! They are holding him hostage. If I do not return the money, they will kill him!"

I knew full well that Audrey would kill us anyways, but we were also responsible for the Greens.

"And I have a responsibility to Britain," said James. "We will help your friend, but you must do it my way!"

He then revealed a plan that was so risky and audacious that I gasped. He wanted Audrey to realise that Leonard and I had failed, and thus force her to retreat. According to James, it was the only chance to get the woman and her cronies to lead us to the anthrax.

"But they will kill Holmes! They want to burn down the house with him and all the evidence!"

"They cannot simply kill him," he said. "They do not know that I am watching them. The fire will look like an accident. If they cut his throat, the investigators would know. If they shot him the bullet would remain in the body. No, I think at dawn they will set the house alight and leave him there to burn. With the proper timing, however, we will succeed in saving Mr Holmes in time, without raising Audrey's suspicion. Our agents will then follow them. With any luck they will lead us straight to the anthrax."

"This is madness!"

"Welcome to the Secret Service," he said, furrowing his brow and finishing his cigarette.

The whole case had grown beyond my comprehension. The Secret Service, chemical weapons, ten-year-old Nazis… What I would give for an old-fashioned murder or embezzlement! The world of crime had changed, perhaps more than anything else.

Meanwhile little Leonard had begun to come to. He straightened up and dusted the shards off of his clothes. Before we could recover, he jumped to the other side of the car, bounded off of it and lunged at James with a wild scream. He leapt right onto his face and thrust his fingers into his eyes, wrapping his legs around the agent's neck like a monkey.

James staggered a few steps back and fell onto the hood of the car, trying in vain to tear the boy off of him.

I searched frantically for a way to help him. My gun lay a few yards away on the road, but it was now useless. The chamber was empty and I had no bullets. I limped to the agent's car and opened the rear boot to see if I could find another weapon.

The boy's thighs squeezed around the agent's neck like a vise-grip. Strangulation was imminent and James was fighting for every gulp of air, trying with all his might to pry Leonard's legs apart.

I could not find anything of use in the car. There was no jack or other blunt object that I could use to club the boy; just a first aid kit and a few bottles of alcohol. Had James been on his way to a party?

"Get down!" James managed to sputter.

Between his fingers he was still holding the cigarette, which he now flicked in the direction of the lorry. It landed in the puddle of gasoline, which immediately caught fire.

A wave of heat hit us. Leonard looked back just as the lorry exploded. The noise rocked the street and the lorry burst into pieces, one of which struck the boy, whom the agent used as a human shield, right in the face.

He squealed, loosened his grip and clutched at his face. The scorching piece of metal was lodged in his face, which had also been scalded by the burning gasoline.

James threw the boy to the ground, but the pain seemed to infuriate him even more. He rolled and jumped to his feet, grimacing and brandishing his fists.

"Spirited boy," said James.

The agent hurried towards the boot, grabbed two bottles, smashed them on the fender and tossed their contents at Leonard. The little creature burst into flames like a torch.

The agent looked at the labels on the bottles.

"Vodka and Martini... Dangerous combination!"

Leonard ran around blindly before he lost consciousness. I pulled a blanket out of the car and threw it on him to extinguish the blaze. With James's help I succeeded. The agent then pulled out a pair of handcuffs and locked the smouldering unconscious boy to a fence.

Then he placed his card on the boy's chest.

"The police will know what it means and what to do with him," he explained.

We could hear sirens approaching. Someone hearing the explosion must have looked out of their window and called the police or the fire brigade, perhaps both. The lorry was still in flames.

On the horizon between the houses we could see that the dark sky was beginning to lighten. In a moment the sun would rise.

"We are running out of time!" I cried.

We hopped into James's Aston Martin. He abruptly stepped on the accelerator and the car took off like a thoroughbred. I clenched the dashboard and held on for dear life.

By the time we reached Audrey's villa the house was already alight. The flames licked the roof and leapt into the dawn sky.

Audrey was gone. The lorry that they had been loading as we left was gone.

There was no sign of the Secret Service agents.

"Where are your men?" I cried.

"We'll figure that out when Holmes is safe," James said. "Perhaps it is not too late."

James stepped on the accelerator and the car smashed through the entrance gate. The metal grille flew into the air and our car skidded to a halt right at the front door.

In the garden the frightened dogs were stumbling about, still drowsy from the ether but terrified of the fire. Their owner had left them to their fate.

They ran toward us. For a moment I was terrified, but instead of attacking us they scurried into the car and ducked beneath the seats, trembling like leaves.

James headed straight for the front door. He unceremoniously kicked it open and acrid smoke billowed through, practically blinding us. The fire seemed to be everywhere; entering the living room was impossible.

"We need to get to the second floor study in order to access the secret room!" I shouted at James.

Despite the advancing flames we headed up the stairs. I was exhausted. I pressed against the wall and crawled up the stairs slowly. I pressed a handkerchief over my mouth and nose, but I was choked with smoke.

The second floor was also on fire. The transverse beams in the hall leading to the children's wing collapsed and fell in pieces on the floor.

I looked around for James, but through the fire did not seem him anywhere.

After a few seconds that seemed like hours he reappeared. He was returning from the study, covered in soot, sweat streaming from his forehead. But over his shoulder he carried Holmes! His hands and feet were cuffed, his face showed evidence of having been beaten, his eyes were closed. I could not tell if he was stunned or dead.

"Go back, Doctor!" the agent shouted at me. "I cannot carry you both!"

He pushed me ahead of him down the stairs. We staggered and stumbled through the grey fog that made the air unbearable, but we finally got outside. At a safe distance from the house we fell to the turf. Just then the lawn sprinklers switched on, soaking us in a cooling shower.

For the third time that night my body announced a shut down and I fainted dead away.

***

When I came to, Holmes was already untied and on his feet. His eyebrows were singed, but otherwise he seemed all right. A weight dropped from my heart.

He and James were discussing the events of the last few hours. The detective described what had happened after I left with Leonard. Audrey, Tanuja and Jeeves had loaded their belongings into the lorry. When we did not return, Audrey fell into a rage and vengefully left Holmes to burn. She lit the fire using the secret documents that proved she was a Nazi spy and these had now been irrevocably destroyed. All that was left of their contents was what the detective could remember. He assured us that it was not inconsiderable and that he would brief us about it at the earliest opportunity.

"Shouldn't we tell Crusher to send a guard to the Greens?" I said.

Holmes noted that I was awake, but as was his habit, did not express much joy.

"Indeed, but I do not think the young lady will make good on her threat, as it would expose her to unnecessary risk," he said calmly, as though we were talking about a radio programme. "It must be clear to her that Leonard probably fell into the hands of the police. Sooner or later he will talk, and then every policeman in the Isles will be after her. She must seek a different revenge."

James nodded, but kept glancing about anxiously.

"I do not understand what happened to my people," he said, scowling. "Even if one team followed Audrey, the other should have remained here to protect you. Where have they gone to?"

He sat behind the wheel of the Aston Martin and pulled a handheld radio transmitter from out of a compartment in the dashboard. He tried to contact with his colleagues, but nobody answered.

"Where were they posted?" Holmes asked.

It could not have been in sight of the house, as they would have been easily discovered. James did not answer and started the engine. The motor coughed stubbornly, but still turned over. We kicked out the trembling Dobermans and Holmes and I wedged ourselves into the passenger seat.

We drove a few blocks until we spied two Secret Service cars parked discretely behind some bushes. Unlike James's Aston Martin they were common variety Fords, the type one sees everywhere.

They were empty.

We stepped out of our car and looked inside. Binoculars, bags of biscuits and magazines lay on the seats. I wondered at their carelessness. But there was no trace of them anywhere.

James went around to the back of the car and grasped the handle of the boot.

It was smeared with something sticky. He looked pale.

He opened the boot and cursed.

"Alex!"

His dead colleague lay inside the boot, twisted in an unnatural position. Below him lay one more agent, who scarcely fit into the boot.

Their throats were cut.

The scene in the second car was similarly gruesome. And next to the dead agents lay the lifeless body of the butler, Jeeves.

Tanuja and her machete had eliminated all witnesses.

James had been wrong about one thing: Audrey no longer cared whether she drew attention to herself. This was a high stakes game that needed an audience. She had played all of her cards and knew that she held the ace.

XI

The Enemy of My Enemy

We had neither the anthrax nor Audrey nor any clue as to where she had fled. But we were not completely empty-handed. At lease we now knew our enemy, and her true motives and intentions.

Over the next few days, Holmes, James and I patiently repeated everything we knew to the interrogators at ever higher levels of the Secret Service. The problem was not that they did not believe us – nobody dared take Sherlock Holmes lightly – but in the sensitivity of the case. Despite all that what we had uncovered, and despite everything that the military had prepared, the politicians still hoped to appease Hitler. I could not help but think of the parallels to the Von Bork case.* The primary interest of the Ministry of Foreign Affairs was to postpone the impending war – or if possible avert it altogether – and not to escalate tensions with the public revelation of a spy in its midst and accusations that the Reich was stealing biological weapons.

Certainly not without evidence.

The most important thing Holmes discovered in the safe of Audrey's villa were the plans for something that Hitler's generals called Operation Pastorius.

It was an act of sabotage and terrorism directed against the United States. The aim was to cripple American industry and to encourage chaos and panic among the civilian population. For Hitler this meant that the Americans would be too busy with their own affairs to participate in the European theatre. For Germany, America was a power that it was best to avoid. At least for now.

From what Holmes had read, the plan was to paralyse the American aluminium and magnesium industries and to destroy cryolite factories. This was to be followed by the detonation of bombs at New York's Pennsylvania and Grand Central stations, at stations in Washington and Chicago, and major department stores owned by Jews. This was to be followed by the destruction of water and electricity supply in New York, the hydroelectric plant at Niagara Falls and the Hell Gate Bridge in New York. It was also presumed that after the attacks the US government would begin to persecute German citizens living in the US, leading to an even greater rallying cry for all pro-Nazi Germans.

Presumably Audrey's role in Operation Pastorius was connected with the anthrax. If it got into the hands of Fascist agents in the US, all hell would break loose. As cruel as it sounds, perhaps it was fortunate that the records and secret plans ended up in Richard's hands. It may have been the watershed moment when he ceased listening to the poisonous words of his beautiful mistress.

"Such odiousness," I said furiously as we discussed the topic yet again at a briefing with James's boss, the director of the Secret Service.

We were in his spacious office above the murky Thames.

"You must warn the Americans of the danger!"

"But only unofficially," said Mycroft's successor.

He lacked Mycroft's aristocratic superiority; his manner was more like that of a kindly uncle. But it appearances can be deceiving; his judgment and ability were second to none.

"Unfortunately these allegations are entirely unsubstantiated. If the German ambassador were to hear about it there would be a scandal."

"If only we knew when and how they intend to transport the anthrax to America," said Holmes, who had fully recovered from his injuries sustained a few nights ago, "we could foil the plot without unnecessary upheaval and without involving the Americans."

"How hard can it be to smuggle such a thing?" I asked.

"For experts it will be easy," said the detective, throwing up his hands. "It is nothing less than a microbe. The cultures are kept in a solution in a vial. It will naturally be sealed airtight, but even so we are talking about an item the size of a golf ball."

"Even if the Americans searched every traveller from Germany, it is virtually impossible to inspect all arrivals," said James. "Never mind the fact that the Reich is building a large fleet of submarines."

"That's not a solution," said Holmes, shaking his head. "We must get the anthrax before it arrives in the United States."

"You realise that it may already be too late..." said James.

"No, I am certain that the anthrax is still in Europe, perhaps even in London," my friend said. "Audrey did not have time to hide it far away. Only a few hours passed between our visit and the time when the Secret Service began watching the house. After that, as we know, no one left the villa and nobody came to pick anything up."

The director looked at a large map of the world, which occupied an entire wall of the office. We were sitting beneath it in low chairs and craned our necks to see if we could find a clue.

"We shall assume for now that the anthrax is still in England."

"Let us summarise the possibilities," said James.

Holmes took a hard candy from a bowl on the coffee table and popped it into his mouth.

"Have you secured Audrey's parents?" he asked.

"Unfortunately no," said the director with displeasure. "They were tipped off and disappeared. Their house is deserted and a substantial part of their assets have been transferred to Switzerland. It is incomprehensible to me that one of the oldest and most respected families in Britain would thrust a knife into our back. And what's more, a family that held a key sector of our industry in its hands! Of course, we will investigate how far back the roots of their betrayal go, but it is a long process."

"Check to see whether your archives contain a record of a person named Tanuja," said Holmes. "Her activities date back about forty years ago to the 1890s."

"The Indian maid who killed my men?" the director asked.

"Yes, we have already encountered her once before."

"Or rather battled her," I corrected Holmes.

"Indeed, the doctor is right," the detective conceded. "She was already thirsty for blood back then, though not mine. In 1894 I prevented the attempted murder of the Queen."

"I am not aware of the incident," said James.

"Naturally. History did not record it. It was deliberately kept a secret, for more than anything it revealed the failure of the Queen's security staff. There was no official investigation or manhunt. But now Tanuja has returned on the scene and is somehow involved with the Nazis."

"We'll check it," said the director. "I am hardly surprised, however, as there are now more and more extremist factions in India who are putting their hopes in Nazi Germany. Their hatred of our rule has led them to seek allies among odious dictators. The enemy of my enemy is my friend. If Indian terrorists sent Tanuja forty years ago and she failed, she will be all the more driven to succeed now."

Holmes also shared his other notes with the director. First, the frequency of Audrey's radio, and then the designation LZ 129, which still haunted our minds. I suspected it would be the key to the search.

"Well," said the busy director. "What else do we have?"

"Leonard," said James, through clenched teeth.

He still had a red mark around his neck, courtesy of the boy.

"Ah yes, the boy" said the director, raising his eyes from the notes and removing his spectacles. "It will be a challenge. Our doctors are baffled by his case."

"Where is he now?" I asked.

The director fidgeted in his chair. He had had no personal experience of Leonard, so he could not help but think of him as a more or less regular boy who had been crippled by one of his agents. The rest of us did not have this problem.

"We are holding him in Cane Hill," he said.

This was a heavily guarded mental institute for the criminally deranged. Holding him anywhere else would be dangerous to himself and to others.

"Did you try interrogating him?" Holmes asked.

"The doctors have not yet permitted it. He is in a bad state and is recovering from third-degree burns. We must wait until his condition stabilises."

"There is no time, sir!" James cried. "Every hour that we waste helps the enemy!"

"You should have thought of that before you set the child on fire!" said the director, glaring at him, "Nevertheless, I shall exert pressure on them."

"If you allow, we will go see him," I suggested. "I know the director of the hospital."

Last I heard the institute was led by Dr George Lilly. I would not call him a friend, more of an associate from the days when I still practised medicine. He had once helped me considerably in a most peculiar case of a patient with Munchausen syndrome. Lilly must have held the post for at least twenty years.

The director of the Secret Service agreed. It was imperative that we learn what we could from Leonard.

"I'll go with you," James offered.

But Holmes refused.

"That's not a good idea. I think you are the last person he wants to see."

Neither the agent nor his commanding office could object to this, and so when we set off the next day, our car was driven by the scowling Steiner. I had no idea why he was in such a foul mood. But as the sky was grey and it rained the whole way, I too fell into a sort of funk and was silent for most of the trip.

Cane Hill was in Croydon, where it majestically overlooked neighbouring Couldstone and the Farthings lowlands. In fine weather the view of Surrey must have been magnificent.

It consisted of several two- and three-story dark stone buildings, with tall windows and a few spires. As our car climbed the hill and the roof of the majestic institute appeared among the trees, a cold chill ran down my spine. It was as though I could feel the madness within those walls in my joints. I did not understand how Dr Lilly could endure it.

We parked the car and Steiner pulled some suit bags out of the boot. I wondered what he had brought them for.

"Excuse me, Watson, I did not consult with you, but I was afraid you might disapprove," he said apologetically. "I have devised a somewhat unorthodox way to interrogate Leonard."

I raised my eyebrows and assured him there was no reason for concern. I had no intention of challenging him.

Dr Lilly was already expecting us. He naturally remembered me, but it cannot be said that his manner was particularly cordial as a result. It was only with great effort that I managed to persuade him to give us access to the burnt and mentally sick boy.

He led us down a long corridor. Patients with sleepy eyes wandered to and fro. We walked through a ward for those patients who did not need special supervision, people suffering from minor problems caused by overwork and stress who simply needed an escape from the modern world and its demands. For these patients Cane Hill served as a sanatorium.

The next wing was only accessible after a security check and several doors needed to unlocked. The patients here were kept in separate rooms and those who moved through the corridors had to be accompanied by orderlies. Their dull, expressionless eyes stared blankly. These were patients with more serious mental disorders who required special care.

Another locked door, separated by bars, led to the ward for the most serious cases. These were the lunatics, the criminally insane, whose minds and souls were irrevocably broken and barely treatable.

I peered with distaste into one of the treatment rooms. It contained a medical chair fitted with straps and tools used for lobotomies and other horrible procedures. I shuddered.

"I did not have time to study them in detail, but the documents that I saw in the safe indicate that Leonard was born an ordinary boy," the detective said as we walked through this hall of horrors. "He was a human guinea pig. The drugs he was injected with gave him superhuman strength and increased his resistance to pain, while also dulling his survival instinct and sense of compassion. He is likely addicted to the booster injection."

"So in addition to being full of hatred for us and suffering the mad agony of the burns, he will be more aggressive due to withdrawal symptoms?" I said. "This is the unorthodox approach that you had in mind?"

The detective said nothing.

Dr Lilly stopped in front of a door. He opened the peephole and looked inside. Then he offered us a look.

Leonard was lying on a bed in a tight room with no windows. There was mould on the cracked plaster. His face was covered in bandages, from which a knot of hair and lower jaw protruded. The eyes, which were now closed, were like two small crescents between the strips of bandages. His arms were fastened to the bed with leather straps; the precaution seemed a strange contrast to his little figure. But it was necessary, as could be seen by the red bruises on his wrists. Obviously he had struggled long and fiercely with the straps.

"He has been tranquilised," said Dr Lilly. "His seizures have become stronger. I must insist that your interrogation be as short as possible."

"Doctor, I give you my word that we will not bother the boy," said the detective. "But would you mind leaving us alone? The information that we hope to obtain is of the utmost sensitivity."

The doctor reluctantly entrusted him with the key to the cell and told the orderly on duty to leave as well.

We were now alone. Steiner laid the suit bags on the floor.

I was eager to find out what Holmes had dreamt up.

"I swore that I would never wear it," said the major frowning. "But if it serves a good cause... I will do it for you, Mr Holmes, for everything you have done for me and my wife, I will make this exception."

He unbuttoned the bag and pulled out his old Wehrmacht uniform.

* *His Last Bow*

XII

The Ends Justify the Means

After he had changed I almost did not recognise Steiner. I knew him as our good-natured manager, but when he put on the tailored uniform of a Nazi major, his expression changed. Gone was his friendliness and joviality, replaced by toughness and intransigence. His already sharp features stood out even more. And when he slowly pulled the cap with the emblem of the imperial eagle clutching a swastika over his dark hair and greying temples, he was a truly fearful sight to behold.

My stomach tightened.

"Where do you intend to go dressed like that?" I asked, gulping.

"The Major has agreed to interrogate Leonard," said Holmes. "Despite his weakened state the boy would certainly recognise us, so I have devised a ruse. I am counting on you, Steiner!"

The retired soldier clicked his heels and straightened his back.

"I am ready, sir!"

The detective reached into his jacket pocket and pulled out a small leather case. He opened it and removed a bottle of clear liquid and a syringe. This was equipment from his days as a drug addict. I had no idea that he was still in possession of it.

Noticing my dismay he patted my shoulder soothingly.

"Do not fear, Watson," he smiled. "It has lost all temptation for me. It is intended for someone else."

This was not very reassuring.

"What is the substance?"

Holmes showed me the bottle.

"A harmless placebo," he said. "Merely a solution of vitamins. We will take advantage of Leonard's desire for the drug. If we can convince him that this is his tonic he will say anything in order to get it. Steiner will make the ruse easier to accept. I am aware of the questionable medical ethics. Sometimes the ends justify the means."

"I would have never believed that we would resort to using a terrifying Nazi officer to interrogate a child," I said, holding the bottle up to the light.

"We must not forget that the creature in the other room has nothing in common with a child besides appearance," said the detective. "There is no trace of childhood left in him. Even before the German doctors subjected him to their experiments he was no ordinary youngster. The evil must have resided in him long before.

Surely they chose him for his innate disposition to violence."

We walked to the door and took a deep breath.

"Whenever you are ready, Major," I said.

"I have experienced more interrogations than you can imagine, gentlemen," he said, frowning. "Both as interrogator and interrogatee. When I eventually questioned the meaningless orders of my superiors the Führer accused me of treason."

That was the first time he had spoken to us of the events that had cast him into exile in Fulworth.

He adjusted his grey-green jacket and stashed Holmes's paraphernalia in his pocket.

"But whatever side I was on it was a dismal process."

I unlocked the heavy cell door, let him in, and closed it behind him. I left open the peephole so that the detective and I could watch what happened.

Steiner turned on the lamp and angled the shade above the bulb so that it shone directly into the boy's face. Then he leaned over and opened the ammonia capsule under his nose. The pungent smell penetrated the bandages and the sleeping goblin slowly began to awaken. The Major also shook him.

Leonard began to whimper in a childlike manner.

"Pull yourself together, you sissy," Steiner barked in German. "Don't you know how to behave in the presence of a superior officer? Or are you the little bastard that you were when we found you?"

The boy trembled and squinted through his bloodshot eyes. He blinked uncomprehendingly at the man bending over him.

"Where am I?" he mumbled.

He tried to raise his hands to block the blinding light, but the straps prevented him.

"The British captured me... sir... I need… it."

"We got you out, kid," the Major said. "At the cost of a great sacrifice. Try to focus now, do you understand me?"

The boy seemed to be only half listening. As the detective assumed he was in a state of semi-consciousness, it must have come as no surprise that he was laying on the same bed in the same room. He believed his native German and the uniform; that was enough. The only thing his brain wanted was the drug. When he was awake, his body demanded it. He was shaking in a paroxysm of withdrawal.

"I need..." he mumbled, barely audibly. "Please... I have followed all orders."

Holmes looked away. He had once been in a similarly deranged state some thirty years ago.

Steiner shook the child roughly.

"Focus! I will give you what you need; but first report!"

"Please, I can't take it anymore..." Leonard moaned. "Give it to me now!"

Steiner now held the bottle in front of him and the boy's eyes brightened. He slowly took out the syringe, pierced the cork and filled the syringe with the solution. Then he squeezed out an air bubble and grasped the boy's arm.

But he did not inject him yet.

"Where is our consignment?" he demanded.

The little Nazi stared at the syringe as though it were a sacred object.

"At the dead drop at Kings Cross Station, exactly according to instructions," he replied. "As soon as Audrey was compromised."

That was a few days ago. This meant that the anthrax could be anywhere by now.

"Who picked it up?" Steiner continued.

Leonard blinked.

"Agent Methuselah," he groaned, looking around in surprise.

The suspicious question pulled him a little closer to reality. Holmes and I withdrew from the peephole in case the boy might accidentally glimpse us.

The Major immediately realised the danger and placed the needle on the boy's forearm. This returned Leonard's attention to the drug. In pursuit of the anticipated pleasure, he ceased to tremble.

"And LZ 129?"

I held my breath in anticipation.

"Ready to start," he said. "The latest reports from Frankfurt have confirmed the commencement of operations as scheduled."

Then he suddenly jerked his arm forward in an effort to drive the point of the needle into his vein. The Major was startled and inadvertently pushed the plunger. He did not give Leonard the whole dose, but enough to make the boy feel that he had gotten what he wanted.

The boy's pupils dilated and his head fell on the pillow.

Holmes opened the door and called to Steiner, who tried to revive Leonard.

The boy did not react.

"It's all right, Steiner. You can give him the rest of the solution and let him sleep. I have learned everything I need to know."

The soldier injected the rest of the solution and took off his cap. He returned to the hall where the detective explained to us what we did not understand. When I heard it, I could not believe that the meaning of LZ 129 had been right under our noses.

We left the wretched ten-year-old boy without ever learning whether the doctors were able to cure him.

Then we went straight to the headquarters of the Secret Service, where we had arranged another meeting with James and his commanding officer.

They were waiting for us in the director's office. The secretary showed us in as the two spies were reading the papers.

"Gentlemen, I bring good news!" cried Holmes. "The secret of LZ 129 is revealed! And with it the mystery of how the Nazis want to transport the anthrax to the USA!"

The director peered over his copy of *The Times*.

"Ah yes, I know," he said.

"How?" my jaw dropped.

James handed us a copy of the newspaper.

"The papers speak of nothing else," he sighed, pointing to an article on the front page.

I stared at a photograph of the pride of Hitler's Germany, the imperial airship Hindenburg. Its designation was Luftshiftbau Zeppelin 129. In less than a week, on 3 May, the largest flying machine ever made would depart on a transatlantic journey from Frankfurt to Lakehurst, USA.

And, according to Holmes, with the stolen anthrax on board.

***

Later that same day, Universal Exports arranged passage for us on board the airship. The possibility of warning the American authorities about the German airship and its cargo amounted to a provocation of war and was still not the preferred option. It was felt that there was still not enough evidence – a mentally deranged serial killer in the shape of a ten-year-old child was not it. The Secret Service therefore opted for a risky plan: to foil the delivery of the anthrax to the United States from within.

We were given the ideal cover story. It had been planned that a representative of the British government would journey aboard the Hindenburg on a diplomatic mission to the United States – courtesy of Reich Foreign Minister Ribbentrop. And it so happened that this representative was none other than the Permanent Under-secretary of State, the Honourable Sir Frederick Fawcett, who was no stranger to us. He had already proven himself once, and we were glad that a friendly face would be on board the enemy vessel. Fawcett was now over seventy and was confined to a wheelchair, but his eyes still shone bright. To avoid raising the suspicions of the German customs officers, we took the place of the four members of Fawcett's entourage.

To tell the truth, although I am discussing this as though it were "our" mission, in fact it was not our task. Ours ended with the unlocking of the motive behind Richard's suicide. We were now caught up in a maelstrom from which it was impossible to escape. We considered carefully whether we should reveal our findings in Fulworth. What a disappointment for all those who believed in our young protégé and saw in him their vision of the big world. We could only draw comfort from the fact that he had regretted his actions and that every young person is the architect of his own life.

The Secret Service naturally sent James to accompany us on the mission. In fact, it was he who insisted that we come along. He appreciated that without Holmes's contributions he would still be sorting through hundreds of employee files at the laboratory, even though his beloved Aston Martin would no doubt be in better shape.

Holmes also insisted that Steiner join us. He felt that if there was another confrontation, our poor physical condition would be a liability. Steiner, on the other hand, could take care of himself.

But this time he refused.

"I cannot go back to the Reich," he said. "They would regard me as a deserter and execute me!"

His wife also did not evince enthusiasm for the idea.

But his knowledge of the environment and language were so essential that with the help of the Secret Service we managed to create for him a completely new identity, which not even an expert could detect as a counterfeit. This succeeded in convincing him to come. The only danger was if we met someone he knew personally. But as he had never worked in Frankfurt and knew none of the German officers who were on the passenger list of the airship, it was determined that the risk was worth taking.

Two days before the departure of the Hindenburg we embarked on an adventure from which we had no guarantee of ever returning.

"We will go through Dover and Calais, from where we will take the train to Frankfurt," said James, handing us our tickets and passports with visas for the Reich. "The four of us will travel together and we will join up with Sir Fawcett at the airport. We all have diplomatic immunity."

"Do not expect immunity to protect us from the meticulousness of German customs officers," Steiner warned with a hint of pride in his voice.

He did not reject his nation entirely; he only condemned those who sought a morbid desire for power in its name. I spoke with him at length on this issue on the train, as we sat in the dining car together. At times, the Major felt that he was betraying his country by helping the British Secret Service, even if by doing so he was saving innocent lives. Our conversation helped him come to terms with these thoughts. His country had been betrayed by those who ruled her now. I hoped that the great German nation that had given the world geniuses like Goethe, Beethoven and Kant would realise this before there was another war. Deep down, however, especially after what we had learned about Hitler's plans from Audrey and her safe, I doubted this would be the case.

The route led through Belgium, where we stopped at the Brussels station for a while. Many passengers got on and got off, which involved a considerable amount of baggage handling. Holmes and I ordered hot chocolate to be brought to our compartment and whiled away the time watching the bustle at the station.

James interrupted our contemplations.

"I would not stick my head out if I were you," he said, pulling the curtains shut. "After all, you are traveling under a false name and do not want to call attention to yourself."

"I have avoided attention all my life," said the detective. "I know how to remain inconspicuous."

"How about a little refreshment?" I said in an effort to ease the tension.

Holmes was accustomed to conducting his own investigations and was uncomfortable giving the reins to someone else, especially someone younger and more resilient physically. These past two weeks had returned him to a world of mental stimulation far beyond that of the card games and tea parties of Cuckmere Haven. It was the classic dilemma of old age.

We returned to the dining car, where Steiner was savouring a coffee and cigar, and joined him for a drink. After all, it was after five o'clock in the afternoon, we had been travelling all day, and tomorrow an endurance test awaited us on enemy territory.

The train started again, in the direction of the German border. It had moved forward again last year, thanks to the ambitions of the Chancellor, whose expansionist policy tested the patience of his neighbours. Although the Versailles Treaty of 1920 had marked the hilly and mountainous ranges around the Rhine where Germany bordered Belgium, France and the Netherlands as a demilitarised zone, the German army had again occupied it and had no intention of withdrawing.

Here towns gave way to nature. In the distance we could see the first mountains rising, forming a natural border between the nations. Behind them loomed the Third Reich.

I savoured my cognac, oblivious to all that was happening in the dining car. My companions' voices as they chatted drifted in and out of my ears like some passing, half heard melody. It took me a while to realise that they had fallen silent.

Before I recognised the voice, I saw a familiar reflection in the window.

"And I was afraid I would not have the chance to settle the score..." said Audrey. She was dressed in a traveling suit and held a small cosmetics purse.

The locomotive whistled shrilly, as though announcing that the end was near.

XIII

The Angel of Death

The dining car was in the middle of the train, which numbered around ten cars. As it was late afternoon it was nearly full. Some were enjoying an afternoon brandy while others had straggled in for an early supper. But our foursome had lost its appetite, poisoned by Audrey's unexpected company.

The evil woman hovered over us for a moment, maintaining her balance as the car bumped and jostled. When none of us reacted, she coughed meaningfully.

"Won't you invite a lady for a drink?" she asked sweetly.

"I do not see a lady," said the detective, who was not in the habit of forgiving assassination attempts.

She laughed.

"Touché, Mr Holmes," she said.

She pulled up a chair from the next table and squeezed in next to us, placing her purse on the table.

"I see no reason not to maintain decorum," she continued, looking around the wagon. "After all, you are all British gentlemen."

"Not I," said Steiner gruffly.

"Without the beard I almost did not recognise you," said Audrey. "It was a very clever move, confronting me with Richard's parents. And I, silly goose that I am, played along with your theatricals."

"It appears not very well," James interjected.

"Excuse me, we do not know each other yet," she chirped. "You must be the secret agent who deprived me of my brother."

"I doubt he is your brother," he said. "And if so, I do not envy you his blood."

"In our organisation we are all brothers and sisters," she said, waving at the steward from whom she ordered a coffee and a glass of sherry.

"Actually," she said, stopping the steward as he was about to leave with her order. "Bring us a bottle of schnapps. It is time to change old habits and begin to explore new ones."

When the steward left, silence descended over the table, disturbed only by the clinking of the silverware, muffled conversation from neighbouring tables, and the melodic clacking of the cars. The detective drummed his fingers on the table and slowly sipped his brandy.

"How did you find us?" he asked.

"An ear here, an eye there... I am not the only mole in your system, Mr Holmes. We know very well that Leonard divulged how and when Operation Pastorius will be implemented. Naturally I am here to help prevent its disruption. There are more of us who believe in our ideals."

"Too many, unfortunately..."

"My dear Steiner, I pity you," she said, returning her gaze to the Major. "I know all about you. I had your file sent to me. A bearer of the Iron Cross First Class for gallantry during the Battle of the Piave River. A hero of the Ludendorff Offensive. You could have held an important post on the Chancellor's staff had you not succumbed to the delusions of radical subversives and traitors."

"No, that was not what I fought for."

"I suppose I know what you mean," she mused. "We both feel misunderstood by our homeland. Clearly we were both born in the wrong cradle."

"What has Britain done to you?" I asked.

She ignored me and addressed her answer to the Major.

"I envy you your Chancellor; he is strong, decisive, authoritative, firm in his opinions," she proclaimed. She spoke with a sincere, devoted love, of which Richard could only dream. "Determined to follow his goals to build a true thousand-year Reich in Germany. And us? Until recently we ruled an empire. But now whenever it seems that it can't get any worse, it does. A degenerate monarchy, a stuttering king* and an idiot prime minister**. We lose one dominion after another. Healthy families, like mine, are oppressed by liberals and communists. My country is falling apart. In many ways, gentlemen, I am more patriotic than you. I just see farther than you do. The British Empire is dying, but it is not too late to build the foundations of a new empire. Who among us was right and who was wrong will be judged one day by the almighty in heaven!"

She raised her glass in a toast and drank.

None of us followed her example.

"I thought the Nazis did not believe in God," said James.

"Not at all. But we see God differently and elsewhere."

The collection of angels in her London villa suggested she was no infidel. On the other hand, she had casually let it burn to the ground. Perhaps her faith had changed.

"For instance?"

"Personally, I feel closer to the concept of Valhalla," she mused. "Only fallen warriors may enter. One must prove one's valour! It is not enough just to pray humbly and die."

"I thought it was only for men?"

"It depends on the interpretation, my dear. Only warriors may enter. And I intend to fight for the Reich to my dying breath. If that means that behind Odin I will be accompanied by a sensual Valkyrie, then why not? One should try everything."

I was going to try everything myself. I fumbled in my pocket for my revolver, but once again I had not brought it. This time it was lying in my compartment.

"Watson, whatever do you have that gun for," the detective whispered grumpily. "Next time just leave it at home in a drawer where you can go admire it."

"Excuse me, but I usually don't arm myself for a drink with friends," I hissed.

The Major, who was watching us, rolled his eyes.

Audrey noticed that Holmes and I were fidgeting about and suspended her flirtation with James. It must have been obvious to her that we were up to something, because her smile vanished. She placed her hand on top of her cosmetics purse.

"Gentlemen, allow me to call your attention to the fact that this little purse does not contain just my makeup," she said. "Inside the trinitrotoluene explosive charge, the pin to which I am holding and can release at any time, there is a gas bomb containing a solution with part of the sample that you are looking for. In this respect our scientists are one step ahead of yours. Should I deem fit, I shall blow up this whole train. Those passengers who are not torn up in the explosion will be killed by the anthrax. Although I have nothing against them, and I myself do not wish to die, I will do it with the knowledge that I will be taking you with me, and will thus ensure the success of the operation for the Reich."

We could not take the chance of assuming she was bluffing. The threat appeared very real indeed. We dutifully placed our hands flat on the table, as she instructed. The inclination of the table tipped a few degrees as the train began to climb the mountain terrain.

"Do we all agree that we want the train to reach its destination?" she asked.

We nodded.

"And do you agree that you have already reached your destination? I cannot allow you to raise the alarm. Your mission ends here and now."

All nodded except me.

I was the only one who did not understood what she meant.

"But there isn't any station here..."

The others looked at me as though I was a small child.

"Who said anything about getting off at a station?"

James pulled an old-fashioned pocket watch out of his vest and checked the dial.

"You are wasting your time with us, madam. If we cannot prevent the smuggling of the anthrax on board the Hindenburg someone else will."

"Trying to save your neck, James?" she chuckled. "But of course if there was another option you would not be here. Any attempt besides a discreet act of sabotage would provoke a war."

She was enjoying her moment of triumph.

"Time is money, and you have already cost me too much money," she stood up and grabbed the purse. "Please come with me. If you do what I say the other passengers will be spared."

Holmes picked up the napkin from his lap and dried his lips in a distinguished manner.

"This is madness," he said, but followed her obediently.

The rest of us followed behind him. Audrey led us through the train in the opposite direction of travel. The dining car separated the first-class compartments from the rest of the train, so we first passed through the second-class compartments and continued in the direction of the third-class compartments.

Behind the doors of the dining car Tanuja was already expecting her mistress.

It was obvious that Hitler's misguided servant was leading us to the freight cars at the very end of the train. The girl did not want any witnesses.

We moved through third class, where the passengers were mostly dozing on benches. There were families with children, old people and travelling salesmen. I thought we might meet the conductor, but he did not appear. Either Tanuja had already taken care of him or he was on the other end of the train.

Through the windows we could see evergreen trees, gradually thinning as we climbed. We were in mountainous terrain now and the track was no longer heading in a straight line, but curving along the hillsides and rocky massifs. Some of the corners were quite sharp, so that the train had to brake, making it difficult for Holmes and me to maintain our balance.

Suddenly the detective almost fell, but a passenger helped him back to his feet. Audrey and the Indian watched him with eagle eyes. But if Holmes was attempting a ploy I certainly did not notice anything suspicious.

We walked on until we had left the last passenger cars and were standing at a railing behind a footboard leading to the boxcars. An ordinary door with a barred window led to it, but it was locked with a latch.

"Let's kill them here," said Tanuja in a strong accent. It was the first time I had ever heard her speak English. I also noticed her yellow teeth.

The Nazi spy leaned out and looked back along the train.

"No, someone looking out the window might see. We will go further."

Tanuja's raised her ever ready machete and hacked the latch open with one fierce blow. Audrey went through the door first, and the Indian shoved us behind.

The boxcar was full of baggage and bulky luggage that people could not fit into their compartments piled up against the walls.

It all happened in a flash.

Holmes, James and Steiner must have somehow agreed when I was not looking, because suddenly they all rushed our captors together. The detective and the Secret Service agent rushed at Audrey and flung her over a trunk. She flew several yards and fell to her knees on the floor, dropping the purse with the bomb, which flew between some bags. In a split second James slammed the door behind him and Holmes, cutting them off from Tanuja, Steiner and me. Through the bars I saw my friend jump on Audrey's arm to pin her down.

The Major had just manged to seize the Indian for a split second.

I turned my head just as the blade of her machete whistled past my ear and lodged itself in the door.

"Watch out!" Steiner yelled pointlessly.

I crouched down and covered my head in anticipation of the final blow. But the enraged assassin was not the least bit interested in me. She pried the machete from the door and charged the former soldier.

It was a total dejá vu.

The Major, however, had much more combat experience than Holmes and I, and proved a worthy opponent. He spryly avoided her attacks, which with each miss of the flashing blade became more and more vicious. But her wrinkled arms hid more power than Steiner could drain. The old Indian was pushing him ever further back until he was trapped in a corner at the edge of the platform. Her loose black hair fluttered in the wind like a goddess of vengeance as she whipped about the deadly blade.

She raised her arm to strike what could have been for the Major the fatal blow.

But Steiner ducked just in time. Instead of decapitating him, Tanuja's blade got stuck in the wall. She tried to jerk the weapon loose, but it was lodged too deep in the wood. It slipped out of her hands, and suddenly she was defenceless before the Major. He did not hesitate for a moment.

He kicked her in the kneecaps. I heard a crack and she yelped in pain. She took a lame step back and considered her options. She looked at me, the venerable doctor, who was blocking the already barricaded door, behind which was her mistress, Audrey. On the other side was the Major, reaching for her machete. Her only escape was between the cars connected by rods and iron couplers.

Or from the bottom… I never could have imagined she would be so foolish as to try it.

But she did.

Despite the broken knee she bounded forward powerfully and nimbly pulled herself up over the railing like a monkey and disappeared over the roof of the boxcar. She had lost none of the acrobatic skill that we had seen on display all those years ago at Buckingham Palace.

Steiner swung at the railing.

"We must go after her," he shouted at me. "She must not get to the passengers! She is dangerous."

I looked back through the bars into the boxcar. The battle between Tanuja and Steiner had lasted only a moment; Holmes and James were still struggling with Audrey, looking for the hidden switch to her bomb.

The Major had meanwhile climbed up, with the machete tucked in his belt, and began the chase after the Indian women over the roof of the speeding train. I did not want to remain alone on the platform, but scrambling up behind him was out of the question. Once upon a time Holmes and I had performed a similar stunt, and I had barely survived. I slammed the door of the passenger car, hurried back inside and ran in the direction in which they were headed.

There was a roof hatch in the next car, so I stopped, grabbed somebody's luggage, despite their loud protests, and climbed onto it so that I could peer out through the opening.

Steiner and Tanuja had not gotten far; in fact only to the end of the car. The Indian had not only to contend with her injury and the jostling of the train, but the strong headwinds, as she fled in the direction of travel.

Behind the struggling figures towered majestic mountains. It was a clear spring afternoon, the sky was a bright blue, and the crisp air smelled like pine.

Old Tanuja fought back valiantly, but she had no chance against an armed soldier. Now the situation was reversed, and she was dodging him. He aimed the tip of the machete at her neck and pushed her back step by step. The train was swaying precariously and they had to struggle to keep their balance.

When there was nowhere to retreat, she confronted him face to face. Then she glanced over his shoulder at me, winked, and threw herself from the roof into the gap between the cars.

The Major ran to the edge and bent over to look for her. Then he came back to where I was. He lowered himself through the roof hatch, wiped the sweat from his brow and cursed in German. When the passengers discovered that he was German they immediately lost interest in us and acted as though we did not exist. In this part of Europe, near the German border, being German meant automatic deference.

"Is she dead?"

"She must be," said Steiner, breathing hard. "She disappeared beneath the wheels."

"We should go back to Holmes," I said.

My friend's life was still in danger.

We returned to the platform and pounded on the door of the boxcar. The detective's aquiline profile appeared in the window. Once he was assured that it was indeed just the two of us, he unlatched the door and let us in. He was holding Audrey's purse, while James was holding the woman's arm twisted behind her back.

"The Führer will not be satisfied," I told her. "Tanuja has already received her punishment. You, on the other hand, will either have to explain to the Chancellor why you failed or face a trial in England for treason."

She looked at me defiantly and then fixed her gaze on the wall.

Holmes looked at the detonator that he had confiscated from Audrey. Then he grabbed her by the chin and turned her face toward him.

"How does it open?"

He forced her to look at the purse. Under the cover there was a small rotary combination lock.

"With a code," she hissed.

"What is it?"

She hesitated, but James' applied more pressure to the arm that was twisted behind her back, forcing her to cooperate. Tears were forming in her eyes, the first before us that I assumed were not simulated. Then she uttered a series of numbers.

After entering them the detective bent over the suitcase, wondering what the inside would reveal.

There was a muffled sound, like ticking.

Steiner's eyes widened.

"It's a trap!" he cried and with a sharp movement knocked the device out of Holmes's hand.

It rolled to the wall and the soldier threw us to the ground, covering us with his body. James instinctively protected Audrey in the same way.

Then the purse exploded.

* George VI. He was crowned in May 1937, shortly after the events of this story. For his speech impediment he was dubbed the Stammering King.

** Neville Chamberlain, British Conservative politician and prime minister from May 1937.

XIV

The Hindenburg

The explosion ripped a huge hole in the wall of the boxcar. Debris showered over us and we could feel the wind and hear the roar of the rear locomotive. The bomb also ripped a hole into the loading ramp, some six feet high and ten feet wide, so that if we had the time and inclination, we could admire the panoramic view of the mountains and the Rhine at the bottom of a chasm that we would soon cross over an iron bridge that was visible in the distance in a bend in the track.

The Major, who had covered us with his body, had been hit by the blast right in his back. In so doing he had probably saved our lives. Although it was not a big bomb, a frontal impact would have liquidated us. He fell over us, lying on the ground and moaning in pain.

When Holmes and I flipped him over I knew why. Instead of a back he had bleeding shreds. Burned pieces of clothing mixed together with singed skin and flesh. He gurgled in agony, which at the same time kept him conscious. The injuries were not life-threatening, but at the moment we had no way to help him.

I myself was afraid to breathe because I was worried about the anthrax, which Audrey claimed the bomb had contained. I had an experimental vaccine hidden in my suitcase in our compartment, but I had little desire to test it on myself. Of course, it was a senseless reaction brought on by panic. Had the bomb indeed sent anthrax into the air, nothing would have helped us.

James tumbled to the ground with Audrey in a strange dance. They were fighting with one another, trying to break free from each other's grasp. It was a ferocious battle, in which neither spared the other. There was no place for gentlemanly conduct in a fight over the fate of the world and the Secret Service agent held nothing back. But the Nazi held her own. Apparently she had undergone combat training, so she gave as good as she got.

I wanted to toss James Tanuja's machete, which the Major had dropped during the explosion and was now a few feet away from me, but I missed the mark. I kicked it too hard and it spun and flew past the agent and out of the car.

Holmes crawled on his knees to the point of the explosion and studied the debris of the bomb. He thoroughly examined it piece by piece. From out of the corner of his eye he watched James, who was trying to keep the spy in the corner.

"Bluffing!" he exclaimed. "I think it was an ordinary bomb. I find nothing to suggest that it contained an anthrax capsule!"

I was relieved. On the other hand, it meant that the whole batch was ready to do harm elsewhere.

Audrey snarled like a cornered beast. She had nothing to defend herself with except for a pair of heavy suitcases. She and James crouched against each other, both ready to lunge. Audrey knew that she had nothing to lose. Both options, which we had indicated to her when she had lost control of the situation, were unacceptable for her. At home she would be punished for treason, in the Reich as a failure.

An enemy who has nothing to lose is the most dangerous.

She threw herself at the agent and pushed him with all her might. He clutched at her, but she was determined to keep moving forward towards the hole in the train. The train had now arrived at the bridge and was panting through the pass to the other side, where Belgium ended and the occupied Rhineland territory began. Audrey intensified her pressure, propping her feet on joints on the floor of the boxcar. The agent struggled. To avoid falling out of the train he had to stop the vicious girl completely. It was either him or her.

He kicked his knee against her stomach. The blow weakened her momentarily. It was just enough time for James to pull his gold pocket watch out of his jacket and break the chain loose from its clip. With a flick of his wrist he turned the chain into a noose around Audrey's neck and pulled.

She gasped and her eyes bulged. She tried to snatch at the noose, but as she reared, the metal chain cut into the skin of her neck even more. She clawed at his hands and kicked her legs wildly, but he did not release his grasp. I thought about poetic justice. She was experiencing what had killed our dear Richard.

James did not intend to strangle her to death. He held onto her just long enough for her to lose consciousness.

But she had her own plans. Before she lost consciousness, in a last convulsive attempt, she tried again to push the agent from the train. He ducked, and at that moment released the watch chain and clutched at the torn wall of the boxcar to stay inside. But Audrey was propelled forward by her own momentum and fell from the car into space. James tried to grab her, but his hands just grazed the tips of her fingers.

She vanished from our sight.

Holmes and I rushed to the agent's side. We leaned over and saw the spy beneath us like an angel with cut wings plummeting from the bridge into the depths below. She made no sound as she fell to her doom, probably because James's golden garrote was still tightening around her neck. The whipping wind brought tears to our eyes. It was the only sympathy she could expect from us.

"Give my regards to Valhalla, Fräulein!" said the agent.

I shuddered.

But I did not have much time to come to my senses. As Audrey fell into oblivion, we heard footsteps and angry shouts on the roof above our heads. Then stick-thin black legs suddenly swung in through the hole and locked around James's neck. Tanuja had survived to avenge her mistress! The Indian tensed her leg muscles and ripped the agent out of the train.

There was no helping him.

He yelled and reached to us, but his cries were drowned out by the roaring of the wind.

Down he plunged into the abyss; and with him our chances of successfully completing our mission. I closed my eyes, unable to watch.

Thankfully Holmes remained on the alert, as Tanuja was still intent on blood. He quickly grabbed her ankle that was hanging from the roof and pulled the Indian into the boxcar. She tried to resist, but there was nothing for her to hold onto on the roof, and she slid and tumbled down.

When fleeing from Steiner she must have jumped between the cars, but she had obviously injured herself doing so, as her face was bloody and torn and she was missing a few teeth.

Even in this sorry state she managed to put up a fight. As she fell into the car she brutally kicked the detective in the face. He released her, and this was Tanuja's undoing. At that moment the train leaned into a sharp curve and the old woman teetered on the edge of the hole for a moment before losing her balance and falling out.

But she did not fall into the chasm, which was already behind us. Instead she landed on the embankment right next to the track. As she staggered to her feet the wheels of the last car caught the edge of her billowing skirts and literally sucked her under the rear locomotive, which crushed her beneath it, leaving a red mush behind on the tracks.

In a matter of moments we had rid ourselves of two enemies, but also lost our two closest allies. The badly wounded Steiner could no longer be of service to us. And poor James... I cannot even tell you how deeply shaken I was by his death.

The detective must have realised that I was in a panic and tried to cheer me up.

"Perhaps he survived, Watson. I am a living example that even a vertiginous fall may not end tragically," he said, recalling his experience of the Reichenbach Falls.

But I highly doubted that the trickle of water at the bottom of the pass, which could barely be seen from above, could have saved the agent.

We stumbled over to the Major, who was barely conscious. There were large beads of sweat on his forehead. I instructed Holmes how to look after him and rushed to our compartment for my medical bag. Along the way I finally came across the conductor, whom I discreetly sent to the boxcar. If the detective's plan were to succeed, we could not cause pandemonium among the passengers, a number of whom were German. Fortunately, our skirmish had occurred at the tail end of the train and hopefully no one had seen or heard anything.

Thankfully the French crew of the train from Calais were persuaded to cooperate. They were aware of the threat from the common enemy. The erudite and sophisticated engineer listened to Holmes and connected with his dispatcher over the radio. He left us in suspense for a few minutes before he connected with the embassy and obtained proper permits and certificates.

So for now we could breath easy. There was one last village station before the German border. The train therefore made an unscheduled stop there and discreetly disconnected the damaged boxcar, which, had it been seen, would certainly have caused unwanted questions.

Meanwhile Holmes and I got off the train and arranged an ambulance for Steiner. We said goodbye to the good Major and believed that we would meet again.

Then we boarded the train once again and set off for the carefully guarded border of the Third Reich.

***

No pictures or pamphlet could have prepared me for what I saw at the Frankfurt airport. We had already spent the previous night in the city, and although the flight was scheduled for eight o'clock in the evening, we went during the day to the airport to take a look around.

The members of the ground staff were just bringing the gigantic airship out of the hangar. It was as tall as a fifteen-storey house! There was no need for any cranes or towing equipment; only a few dozen, maybe a hundred men. Divided into groups, they dragged the ship behind them on tow ropes. They moved along the narrow cobblestone paths and behind them the most beautiful creation of avionic engineering that I had ever seen hovered.

The airship was shaped like a giant cigar. The May sun shone on its stately, silver-grey hull, beneath which protruded a longitudinal rib structure. The name of the craft was written in ornate Gothic Germanic lettering in red followed by the registration number D-LZ 129. The upper and lower tail rudder blades attracted my attention with their giant black swastikas in a white circle on a red background. The same flags were posted far and wide. Judging by their frequency, as I had noticed on the way from the station to the hotel and then to the airport, they were throughout the country.

Beneath the shell I saw several sets of windows belonging to the two passenger decks. The cabins were sunk inside the hull for better aerodynamics. At the front there was a small wheelhouse with views in all directions. I had no doubt that we were in for a unique experience. The ship was powered by four diesel Daimler-Benz engines with an output of 890 kilowatts capable of moving the monstrous vessel at 84 miles per hour, placed in pairs on the sides of the torso.

The men dragged the ship to the widely set anchor masts and tied her.

Holmes watched the operation with great interest, as did dozens of onlookers who admired the Hindenburg from behind the fence. Over the last few nights he had carefully studied all available information about the airship, and like I he was captivated by the sight of it.

"We must not forget that this is a hostile arena for us," I said.

"You might disagree, my friend, but this will probably be my most impressive opponent," he said, shielding his eyes from the sun and studying the machine in all its glory.

"Too bad that something like this is used to promote the Third Reich," I regretted.

"Hitler came to it by sheer accident," said the detective. "Its mission, as was the dream of the father of the airship Count Zeppelin, was to unite nations. Nor is the current head of the company, Dr Hugo Eckener, a true

Nazi. Unfortunately, the programme of transatlantic flights was essentially nationalised; commercial flights are operated under the auspices of the German Ministry of Air Transport, Lufthansa, which is the national carrier, and the Zeppelin Company itself only has a one-third share in it. Eckener is therefore powerless."

We slowly walked around the fence and made our way through the onlookers, among which were a number of reporters.

"Where will we meet Fawcett?"

"At the check-in terminal," the detective said.

We still had time.

"It will be like looking for a needle in a haystack," I said, measuring the vessel's impressive dimensions.

"Like a needle in a haystack made from grass mowed on three football pitches," he said. "The Hindenburg is almost as big as the Titanic. It is 800 feet long, 442 feet in diameter and weighs 240 tons. An object the size of a golf ball may be hidden anywhere within it."

"Do we have the passenger manifest?"

"Certainly, it is freely available," he said. "I went through it all night; but there is no name that would cause suspicion."

"How many passengers will fly with us?"

"If nothing changes, we will be joined by a total of ninety-seven people. Thirty-six passengers and sixty-one crew members."

"That is almost two crew members per passenger!" I cried.

"However, it corresponds to the exorbitant price of the ticket," he said, noting that the Secret Service had paid our airfare, which otherwise would have cost us more than we paid for our car. "The Germans want the Hindenburg to be synonymous with luxury."

"So was the Titanic and we know how that turned out," I said.

"Do not worry, Watson. I have been assured that Zeppelins are safe. So far they have flown without incident and there is no reason for concern. The Hindenburg itself made seventeen flights across the ocean last year, ten to the USA and seven to Brazil. There is nothing to crash into in the air!"

With these thoughts we returned to our hotel for lunch.

Later that afternoon we came back to the airport, where we were joined by our escort, Frederick Fawcett. Gone was the athletic blond man full of vigour that I remembered from our meeting with Queen Victoria. He was now confined to a wooden wheelchair and had grown long grey sideburns and wore a pince-nez. A Shetland blanket was draped over his legs and on his lap he held a restless Jack Russel terrier wearing a decorated collar.

Truth be told, he was rather surprised when just two of us greeted him. He had expected two more members of the team. We explained to him what had happened on the way to Frankfurt and how we had lost the more physically capable members of the expedition.

"This is very unfortunate, Mr Holmes," he said, shaking his head anxiously. "If our opponent turns out to be physically fitter than us – which I think is a certainty – I do not know what we will do."

"On board the airship he will have nowhere to escape," I said.

"Then I hope that you will push my wheelchair fast enough," he said, motioning to his assistant.

But Sherlock Holmes released the young man and grabbed the handles of Fawcett's wheelchair himself. He pushed the government official to the gate of the departure terminal.

"We shall do what I have devoted my whole life to," he said. "Instead of force we shall use guile and my powers of deduction."

XV

The Four Thousand Mile Long Investigation

Although the airport departure terminal was surrounded by crowds of people, inside it was surprisingly peaceful. And why not, when only passengers had access, of whom there were only a handful. The detective told me that those thirty-six passengers were only half the capacity that the ship was able to transport. On the return journey, however, the ship was to be filled to the last seat, because many dignitaries would be heading to Europe to attend the coronation of King George VI and Queen Elizabeth.

To avoid all doubt about who was in charge, several SS men in black uniforms and red bands with swastikas above their elbows were milling about. A portrait of Hitler hung in a place of honour in the hall.

Holmes pushed Fawcett to the check-in counter, while the secretary's assistant and I kept in tow. The detective took all of our passports and tickets and gave them to the SS officer behind the desk. The man compared them to his records with an important-looking expression and eyed us suspiciously.

"Your party, sir, should number five people," he said to Fawcett in German, uttering the English word *sir* with slight disdain. "But I see only three men here. Do you want to wait for the rest of your party to check in?"

"My itinerary was arranged at the last minute," said Fawcett. Naturally he left out the fact that the itinerary had been changed by Tanuja's machete and a Nazi spy with explosives. "Our party is complete. There is no need to wait for anyone."

The SS officer frowned. We swivelled around unhappily in his chair, took the documents and went to the office of his superior. There was a heated discussion behind closed doors that lasted for about five minutes.

I was sweating.

"Stay calm, my friends," Holmes whispered. "Worse comes to worst, we are protected by diplomatic immunity. Nothing can happen to us."

"I am not sure whether that means anything to them," said Fawcett.

As if anticipating a problem, two SS men approached our group and stood guard nearby. Fawcett's terrier began to growl and bark. They looked at her with amusement, but did not leave. The secretary grabbed the dog by the collar and calmed her down, perhaps so that she would not jump on the soldier – it would certainly qualify as assaulting a public official. The officer had probably failed with his boss because he returned with a dejected look.

"The forfeited ticket will not be refunded," he informed us.

We assured him that we had not anticipated it would.

"Your passports will be kept with us until we land at Lakehurst," he continued. "Mr Fawcett has a first-class cabin. The dog, however, must go in a special section of the cargo bay at the rear. I assure you that it will be well cared for."

Fawcett grudgingly consented and gave the dog to a member of the ground crew, who stuffed the animal in a crate and hurried off with it.

"The rest of you have standard quarters," he said, handing us boarding passes.

He was referring to the two-person cabins, but since I was to share mine with Holmes, it was all right.

The check-in officer then referred us to his colleague for customs inspection. Our immunity was worthless here, as could have been expected. The SS thoroughly rifled through our baggage, down to the smallest pockets of our toiletry bags.

"It is for your own safety," said the customs officer. "There must be nothing on board the ship that could cause a static discharge."

Before I could protest we were directed to yet another officer, who made a careful record of our weight. It was bothersome, but I had to admit that these measures excluded the possibility of a serious accident.

"It also suggests that the agent who is smuggling the anthrax is in cahoots with the authorities," the detective said. "Otherwise it would be uncovered in the course of these inspections."

From the passenger terminal we went straight to the grassy area where the airship was moored. A choir of Hitler Youth in white knee socks, black shorts and sandy brown shirts accompanied by a brass band was singing *Deutschland, Deutschland über alles*. A flood of Nazi flags waved. It was like being in a newsreel produced by the propaganda ministry.

Some of the other passengers were already waiting beneath the vessel. There were a few Englishmen and several Americans and Swedes, but most of the passengers were wealthy Germans. The sun was slowly getting less bright as the afternoon turned into evening and the start hour approached. Then the huge bottom of the airship opened, and down came two boarding ramps with ladders.

Two crewmen hurried down to help Fawcett and wheeled him to the loading platform, which was the only way to get him aboard. The rest of us climbed into the bowels of the Hindenburg via the steep boarding ramp.

Immediately upon entering we were greeted in the small hall by a bust of President Hindenburg*, after whom the ship had been named.

"Apparently Hitler was furious when he learned that the chairman of the board of the Zeppelin Company named the ship after the late statesman," the detective whispered to me. "He wanted this example of German ingenuity to be named after him."

"That's all we need, a flying Hitler!" someone said behind us.

We wheeled around, startled. Behind us a little man was climbing the steps into the aircraft. He was not young, but was very nimble. He clambered up swiftly, put down his suitcase and buttoned his jacket.

"Careful or a German will hear you and all hell will break loose," I said.

This fanatical nation was sensitive to jokes about their leaders, and I did not want us to come under the scrutiny of the crew.

He literally burst out laughing.

"Too late!" he exclaimed. "Let me introduce myself. Joseph Späh, at your service!"

"You are German?"

"Part German, part Belgian," he replied, bowing. "World traveller, immigrant, acrobat, humourist and artist. I have long been living in the United States, where one breathes easier."

We moved deeper into the ship so as not to block the narrow inlet for other boarders and shook hands with the acrobat. He revealed that he had cancelled a performance for Hitler to take the airship home.

"You have no reason to be shy in front of me," he added, before hurrying off to his cabin.

"Strange man," the detective said.

I suppose the first-class cabins were more impressive, but ours was tiny, just a few square feet, and virtually devoid of furniture. The bed, which was bolted to the floor, was of the bunk variety. There was no reason to linger here, so we went on a first tour of the ship.

Passengers could move freely on two decks connected by stairs. In the middle of the upper deck passengers lined the sides of the common areas – the restaurant on the port side and the observation deck and lounge to starboard. The vessel even had its own post office from which one could send telegrams during the flight.

On the lower deck there were wash basins, a room for the crew, and to my surprise even a smoking room! But a cigar had to wait. It was nearing eight o'clock, and we wanted to watch the lift-off.

The lounge was already filled with passengers, including our companion Fawcett and his assistant. Apart from them and Späh we did not know anyone. Outside it was dark and flood lights were aimed at the Hindenburg. The passengers waved from the windows as camera bulbs flashed down below.

Through the window I heard the captain call out instructions from the wheelhouse.

"Prepare for lift-off!"

The ship undocked from the anchor mast and the ground crew untied the rope, which was stretched to breaking point. The captain ordered the lift-off and several dozen technicians on the tarmac made every effort to help the vessel off the ground. The rest of the work was done by the great ship itself.

Slowly, majestically it soared into the sky until the people beneath us dwindled and disappeared. When we reached an altitude of about 820 feet, the machinist activated the quad propeller engines, which began to move the ship forward.

The Hindenburg headed from Frankfurt to the French coast, and from there was to continue over Ireland to the Atlantic. The British government did not want the ship to fly over its territory, perhaps due to fears of espionage. Despite the slight detour, the vessel would accomplish the nearly four thousand mile long journey in just seventy-two hours!

That was how much time we had to thwart the delivery of the anthrax to the United States.

All that could be seen on the ground down below was lights. Large clusters of yellow dots were cities, smaller ones towns and villages. It was amusing to watch the magical world from this new perspective, until the tenth hour arrived and it was dinner time. The detective had been waiting for it impatiently, as it was one of the best opportunities to get to know the other passengers.

While the walls of the observation deck were covered with white wallpaper and one had a map of the world painted on it, the walls of the restaurant were a yellowish colour and were decorated with paintings of the memorable journeys of Count Ferdinand von Zeppelin to South America. As throughout the ship, here too the interior was strictly functionalist with furniture made of the lightest possible materials. The table and chair frames were made of aluminium, and only the seats and backrests were upholstered.

The chief steward directed our group to a six-person table with a nice view. He could not have picked for us better company than a talkative journalist couple from Berlin, who over dinner eagerly told us all about the other passengers on board.

For instance, at the table next to us was a couple with three small children, the Doehners. Apparently Mr Doehner was an influential businessman from Mexico City. Then there was the owner of a well-known food company Teekanne Rudolf Anders, Danish businessman Hans Vinholt, American fashion designer Philip Mangone and an Italian noblewoman and heiress of considerable wealth, signora Margaret Mather.

Holmes's encyclopaedic brain committed all this information to memory so that he could thoroughly analyse it later. We also met with the crew and commanding officers, who, though they had their own dining room on the floor below, came to introduce themselves to us. The captain was Max Pruss, an experienced officer who had flown airships for many years. He was joined by the famous Captain Ernst Lehmann, who was somewhat older, but was only an observer on this journey.

After dinner we headed to the clubhouse, where our conversation with the pilots continued. Of the two, I found Lehmann to be the more congenial. It soon became clear that Pruss was a loyal follower of the Führer, while Lehmann avoided talking about politics altogether. Indeed, Lehmann was even wearing civilian dress, while Pruss had squeezed his portly body into a ceremonial navy blue uniform with gold braiding. He appeared somewhat jealous of Lehmann and delighted to now be in command. But there was no doubt about either man's professionalism.

Holmes and Fawcett were a receptive audience and let both men speak at length about the construction of the ship. There was plenty to brag about. For Holmes this all had a criminological interest more than anything else. He believed that the more he knew about the ship, the better our chances of unearthing something during the journey.

We learned that the Hindenburg had a duralumin skeleton, composed of fifteen circular counters the size of a Ferris wheel, among which were sixteen cotton bags filled with one hundred ninety thousand cubic metres of gas. The outer shell was made of cotton mixed with reflective materials, which protected the gas bags inside from ultraviolet and ultra-red radiation that could damage and overheat it.

"In fact, if it were not for the British we might not even be here," Pruss said.

I nodded and expressed thanks for their acknowledgment of the contributions of our British engineers. But Pruss began to laugh, for I had unwittingly fallen into the trap that the captain had set for me.

"Indeed we are truly grateful to your engineers," he giggled. "Part of the design is in fact made of duralumin, which was left in the debris from your airship R101. Years ago Zeppelin bought it for eleven thousand pounds from your government!"

Fawcett coughed. The tragic accident in October 1930 did not seem to us a fit subject for humour. It soon occurred to the Germans, especially Lehmann, who discreetly nudged the laughing Pruss in the ribs. We therefore changed the topic of conversation, and after a while the captain excused himself and stated that he had duties to attend to on the bridge.

We were left alone with Lehmann, who rubbed his receding hairline and raised a glass of wine in a toast.

"May our mission, whatever it may be, be brought to a successful conclusion."

We had to agree with that. We drank and could only praise the fine selection of French and German wines on board. In this pleasant frame of mind we continued to converse. Lehmann was not supposed to be on this journey, especially following a tragedy in his family, the death of his two-year-old son. But when the company insisted he agreed. He had been sent to attempt to break the embargo that the Americans had imposed on the export of helium.

He explained that helium gas, which is lighter than air, is relatively rare and extremely expensive. It arises as a by-product of the mining of natural gas in the United States, and is produced nowhere else in the world. But the Americans guarded it heavily and reserved it for use in American airships, not wanting to supply it to a potential enemy. The Germans, on the contrary, were desperate to acquire helium for their airships. Helium, unlike the hydrogen with which the Hindenburg and other German ships were filled, is incombustible.

"When building the Hindenburg our engineers assumed that we would manage to break the embargo and obtain a licence for helium, but we had to change plans," said Lehmann. "Of course, hydrogen also has its advantages. It is much cheaper than helium and as it is lighter it has about ten percent higher buoyancy, freeing up space for more cabins."

"How reassuring," I said.

The captain downplayed my concerns.

"We have years of experience using hydrogen in airships," he said. "There is no cause for alarm. I am sure you have noticed that we even have a smoking room here. And the ship is equipped with security elements to avoid a fire in case of a gas leak."

"Hence the fear of static electricity!"

"Exactly," Lehmann said. "The ship must not contain anything that would cause a spark."

"Do you believe that the government of the United States will lift the embargo?" Fawcett asked.

"It is a real possibility," said the captain. "I have prepared a proposal in an effort to convince them. We would like a helium-hydrogen mix to save as much helium as possible. In practice, this would mean that ship buoyancy would double. There would still be hydrogen inside, but a layer of helium around it acting as a shield."

We acknowledged that it was a brilliant idea, but Holmes was no longer listening. He was watching a man who was sitting alone in the now almost empty lounge within earshot of us, but was acting as though he was not listening.

"Do you know who that is?" the detective asked Lehmann quietly.

The captain, who was sitting with his back to the man, looked around and then grew pale.

"I am not saying anything secret, but even so, I could get in trouble for discussing our aerospace programme with you," he said, lowering his voice. "That man is a member of the Gestapo."

The man noticed that we had lowered our voices because of him. He glared at us, took a last sip of coffee and left without a word.

"Hitler is very protective of his airship..." said Fawcett.

"That is not why he is on board," sighed Lehmann. "To hell with it; I trust you, and anyway, it cannot make matters worse."

Then he leaned over conspiratorially and said: "We've had a warning that someone might try to sabotage the ship!"

* Paul von Hindenburg was a German field marshal, an outstanding figure of the First World War and president of Germany from 1925–1934.

XVI

The Wind Picks Up

It was like being in a chess game without knowing what piece or even what colour you were. My head was racing with what Lehmann had told us. Was the Gestapo man here as insurance in case Audrey failed? Was it part of the game of cat and mouse between the English and German secret services? Was the threat of sabotage a real danger for the ship and its passengers or just a red herring?

We went to bed with a head full of questions. Naturally I could not sleep. Conspiracy or not, it was my first time sleeping a thousand feet above the ground, and I felt airsick. There was a strong headwind from the approaching thunderstorm and lying here on my back was pure torture. Holmes, on the other hand, appeared to be sleeping soundly, judging by the regular sound of breathing from his bunk.

I put on my shirt and trousers and went for a walk.

Both lounges were empty as it was between three and four o'clock in the morning. I therefore went down to the washroom on the lower deck and splashed some water on my face. This made me feel a little better.

Then I heard an unusual noise. One produced neither by the machinery of the ship nor by the raging elements outside.

Silently I opened the door of the washroom and looked out. In the corridor a few yards ahead of me someone stole past quickly in the dark. I could not tell who it was, but he was not wearing a uniform, so it must have been one of the passengers.

But where could he have gone? The engine room? The direction in which he went was off limits to passengers; there was no reason for him to go there.

Strange.

I quickly turned off the light in the washroom before the sliver of light through the doorway gave me away. Curiously I watched where he was going.

The man – I was sure it was a man – had now left the passenger area and was creeping up the metal stairs leading into the bowels of the ship.

It was pointless to alert someone on duty. I decided instead to follow the prowler. Where would he lead me? Wherever it would be, I decided I would not interfere. I was unarmed and had no means of defence. This time, however, it was not my fault. Naturally my revolver had been confiscated and was now being stored in a safety container, as no firearms were allowed on board.

The stairs on which I followed the man led to a narrow maintenance footbridge. It ran through the ship to the very stern, passing through various sectors filled with balloons. Above our heads there was another footbridge. Altogether there were several, connected to each other by ladders, to allow servicemen to quickly get to the point where a failure might occur. Only crew members were allowed access here.

Among the rigging, braces and bulkheads there were few places to hide, and I had to watch my step carefully. There was nothing beneath the footbridge, and were I to fall, I would fly through the outer shell and bring down the entire ship. My heart was pounding, but at least I no longer felt airsick.

So I watched where I placed my feet and for a moment let the man out of my sight. When I looked up again, he was gone. He must have turned into one of the cargo spaces, which extended aft. I quickened my pace to catch up to him.

Suddenly someone stepped in my path. He emerged like a shadow from the cramped space behind the partition and grabbed my sleeve. It was a wonder I did not cry out.

"What, can't sleep?" the man said calmly.

It was Späh, the little man who had ridiculed Hitler. Surely he was not smuggling anthrax for the fascists. Could he be the one whom the Gestapo were after?

"Passengers are not permitted here, are you aware of that?" I said.

"I am. Are you? Why are snooping around? Are you a secret agent?"

"I saw you sneaking in here and I was curious," I said.

There was no point lying when he had caught me. He did not seem to have ulterior motives.

As if to prove it to me, he grinned and nudged me in the ribs in a friendly manner.

"Let me show you something," he said.

He led me into the cargo bay. Two dogs, Fawcett's terrier and a large German Shepherd with a black and golden coat, were being kept here in small cages. When the German Shepherd saw us it barked and stretched.

"Her name is Ulla," said Späh, leaning toward the cage. "I'm bringing her as a gift for my children. I bribed the principal steward to let me come here and check on her."

He pulled a piece of dried meat from his pocket and stuck it through the bars of the cage. Ulla chomped on it greedily.

In the neighbouring cage Fawcett's terrier stood up, licked the wire door and whined.

"Ah, a companion, they will have fun together," said Späh as the dog licked his face.

He gave the terrier a piece of meat too. Then he led me out again.

We returned to the passenger area and promised each other that we would keep our expedition a secret. I returned to my cabin, but to my surprise Holmes was not in bed.

He returned some fifteen minutes later. He had not bothered to dress, wearing only a robe over his sleeping attire.

"I know that you were not feeling well," he explained. "I heard you sigh and roll over, and then leave. When you did not return, I thought perhaps you were sick. So I went to look for you."

I was appreciated that he was worried about me, but I wondered why I had not seen him.

"I went down to the lower deck and saw you sneaking behind Späh," he explained. "I recognised him by the way he walked. Acrobats have a very specific gate and bearing. You were so intent on him not seeing you that you did not detect what was behind you."

"I suppose I'm not a very good spy," I said.

"How so? You have done remarkably well."

I lay down on my bunk and covered myself with the blanket dejectedly.

"Not only did I fail to notice you behind me, but I failed to prevent Späh from seeing me," I said. "Fortunately, he is not the enemy."

I explained why the little German had been walking about.

Holmes climbed up on the top bunk.

"Indeed, he is innocent," he yawned. "I took advantage of your game of hide and seek to search his cabin."

"You did what?"

"I broke into his cabin," he repeated, as if it were the most natural thing in the world. "Fortunately, he is travelling alone, so I searched his personal belongings thoroughly. I found the licence for the dog, and many other documents. He is returning home after a great acrobatic tour of Europe and Asia. He performed in Moscow for Stalin. His programme is a mix of acrobatics and vaudeville. He also has a number ridiculing Hitler, but he certainly did not perform it in Germany. No, Späh is not the saboteur or the messenger of death that we are looking for."

"Good. So now we have only ninety-six suspects."

"Precisely."

"Do you intend to break into every cabin one by one?" I said, reaching for the light switch and turning it off. "The journey will take two more days, so by my calculation that's half an hour for each. You should get started."

My comment was met by silence.

But then Holmes suddenly sat up again. "Watson, there is a dormant genius within you!" he said.

"I was merely jesting, of course," I said to be sure that Holmes understood.

"Naturally, but you are not far off the mark," he said, climbing down and switching on the light. "Don't you see? We have a member of the most powerful secret police in the world on board! Why not use this to our advantage?"

I had no idea what he was getting at.

"You mean the Gestapo?" I said incredulously. "Isn't that who we are fighting against? How do you get the man to help us?"

He threw up his hands in despair at the poverty of my intellect.

"Think a little," he said. "On the Hindenburg there is an officer of the Gestapo whose mission is to uncover a saboteur or to prevent us from seizing the anthrax. He will certainly be carrying information about all crew members and passengers."

"Naturally," I said. "But he is unlikely to be carrying a list of Abwehr members; or a document stating who has hidden the anthrax and where. Unfortunately the Nazis are not that stupid."

"Indeed," he smiled, thinking I understood where he was headed.

"So what purpose does this information serve?"

I was worried that we would take a huge risk for something that was unlikely to help us.

"It will exclude other suspects," he explained. "Those for whom he has records are potential saboteurs and enemies of the Reich. As you rightly said, the Gestapo will not have records about their comrades from the Abwehr. It is elementary. This time the important thing is not the information that we will find, but what we won't find."

Now I understood his logic. And I had to admit that it was sound.

"How do you want to do it? When?"

He rubbed his eyes.

"The second question is easier to answer: tomorrow. As for how, we must first think. Better to sleep on it."

Whether or not sleeping on it was of any help I am not certain. But at least the storm had passed, the sky was clear, and the ship sailed at around eighty miles per hour below the clouds so we could admire the infinite horizon of the ocean below us. Dolphins could be seen leaping through the foaming waves and in the distance the gleaming walls of glaciers.

At breakfast the company was similar to that of the evening before. Fawcett and his assistant joined us throughout the morning. And from the corner of my eye I noted the constant presence of the Gestapo officer. As the day wore on, Fawcett especially was becoming increasingly nervous. He felt that we were wasting our time and doing nothing to help our cause. But he could not evince his displeasure too obviously, as by doing so he risked us being revealed. I understood his frustration, for I too was at a loss about what Holmes had in mind. After lunch I wanted to spend some time on the observation deck and to bask in the sun like any other pensioner for whom three square meals a day and a crossword puzzle were all that was needed for happiness.

Holmes perked up only after dinner.

"Gentlemen, shall we adjourn to the smoking parlour for a game of cards?" he suggested. "I am dying to smoke. After such a fine meal it would be a sin to go to sleep."

Fawcett slammed the napkin on the table and glared at him.

"Do you know what you are doing? There is no time for idiotic games," he muttered. "I will go back to my cabin. Stay here if you wish."

He dismissed his assistant, who had stood up to push his wheelchair.

"I have a lame leg, not hands," he cried, grabbing the wheels and propelling the chair under his own power.

The startled assistant sat down again. Holmes looked around the dining room.

"We need a fourth player," he said.

Then to my dismay he addressed the ever-present Gestapo officer.

"Would you care to join us, Mr ...?"

"Gruber, Fritz Gruber," said the man with consternation.

He too had not expected to be invited to a game of cards. To save face, however, he agreed and walked with us to deck B.

Along the way Holmes and I exchanged a few clandestine words.

"Shall I distract him while you search his cabin?" I whispered.

"You have hit the nail on the head, Watson," the detective replied with a wink.

The smoking lounge of the Hindenburg was very unusual. For security reasons it was separated from the hallway by a pressurised entrance with an airtight lock, which was supposed to prevent a possible hydrogen leak. Inside the lounge there was a single electric lighter fastened to the table and a steward stood on guard to ensure that passengers did not leave a lit cigarette or pipe. On the walls there were paintings of older airships, such as the hot air balloon of the Montgolfiér brothers, whose first voyage across the sky had been a hundred and fifty years ago.

The lounge was now empty, ideal for a peaceful game of cards. We sat down on the blue padded benches and the game commenced.

Holmes did not even have to pretend to be a bad player. Pastor Whittaker and Dr Conway would have been pleased, because the detective was especially generous in his bets. Gruber won a considerable sum from him and after an hour or two of play appeared to be feeling quite relaxed.

Just after midnight the detective stood up.

"Please excuse me, I must recover from the loss," he said. "I will go to fetch my money and will return in a moment."

Gruber looked up from the cards. But as a fairly high wager now lay on the table he was loath to go.

"I shall probably be going too," he said hesitantly.

"You must at least give us the chance to recoup our losses," I said.

Fawcett's assistant was also losing, but was in no hurry to leave either.

The Gestapo man allowed us to persuade him and we continued the game. I tried to play as slowly as I could without raising suspicion. I pondered each move, carefully weighed each bet, while Gruber became increasingly nervous. He constantly checked his watch and glanced at the door.

When Holmes had been gone half an hour he finally lost patience. He put the money in his pocket and threw his cards on the table.

"I quit," he said. "Your friend is probably not coming back."

I shrugged innocently.

In an effort to entice him to stay in the game I pretended to drop my cards for a moment so he could see what I was holding.

Gruber could not help noticing. He looked at me suspiciously.

"What are you trying to do?" he asked.

"I do not understand?" I said quickly, scooping up the cards and shuffling.

"You had this game in the bag," he cried, leaping from his chair. "You let me win on purpose!"

"I must have misread my cards," I muttered.

He ran to the door, forgetting that he had a lit cigarette in his mouth.

I pictured him finding Holmes in his cabin. We could kiss farewell to our mission and a diplomatic solution to the impending war. The Gestapo officer seized the wheel of the airlock and spun it around. The door swung open and Gruber charged out.

But as he did so he ran headlong into Holmes.

"But, my dear Herr Gruber," said the detective, stopping him and plucking the burning cigarette from his mouth. "You must be more careful. Even a tiny spark can cause a great flame."

He took the stunned Gestapo man by the shoulders and led him back amiably to the table, where he carefully extinguished the cigarette.

His words lingered in the air. Like a spark, they too could set off an explosion.

XVII

St Elmo's Fire

The enraged Gruber shot from the smoking room like a cork from a champagne bottle, bubbling and hissing as he went. Were it possible to slam a pressurised hatch door, he would have done so, but we could only imagine the dramatic effect. Fawcett's assistant, who had no idea what had just happened, just blinked. He understood, however, that we had plenty to deal with, so he bid us goodnight and went to his cabin.

Holmes sat down and lit his pipe.

"I had a feeling it would turn out badly," I said, sighing. "What if he had caught you rummaging through his things?"

"Tomorrow will be a busy day," said Holmes. "We will be under the scrutiny of the Gestapo, because Gruber so far has no other suspect."

"What exactly are we suspected of?"

"The threat of sabotage is real. The German Embassy in Washington received a letter stating that the Hindenburg would end in flames."

"An anonymous tip?"

"No, it was written by a woman who is renowned as a psychic."

"A charlatan," I laughed. "If the Gestapo takes it seriously it says little about their intelligence."

"Hitler is fascinated with black magic and the occult. Nevertheless, the fact that the Gestapo have assigned only one man to the Hindenburg indicates that they do not take the threat too seriously. Of course, Gruber himself will not underestimate anything."

In a way I felt relieved. At first I feared that were we to find the anthrax on board we would never arrive at our destination.

"Did you find what you were looking for in Gruber's cabin?" I asked.

"Yes and no," the detective replied. "That's why I stayed so long. Gruber has a briefcase containing documents about every last man aboard, except our group."

"That's understandable," I said. "The two of us are traveling under assumed names, and Fawcett and his assistant are government officials. Fortunately this suggests that the Germans do not have anyone planted within our government."

"I do not agree with your conclusion," said Holmes, shaking his head. "Audrey said that she is not working alone."

"Maybe she was bluffing," I suggested. "After all she kept us at bay with explosives and fictional anthrax. Why not lie about this? She was just playing with our minds."

The detective disagreed.

"No. She had to have learned from someone that Leonard had talked. She also knew that we were heading to Frankfurt and what train we had boarded. Only a few people in the Secret Service and Fawcett knew about our plans. No, Watson, I fear I have found exactly what I was looking for, awful as it may be."

The import of what he was saying was shocking.

"Fawcett's assistant..." I whispered. "It's the only possibility. The boy is the same age as Richard was. Perhaps Audrey beguiled him with her feminine charms!"

"It makes sense," the detective mused.

I thought about the boy. He was so shy and inconspicuous that hitherto I had not paid the slightest attention to him. Were it not for the card game when we needed him as a decoy, I probably would never have entered into conversation with him.

Even when he stood in front of us, he was practically invisible. A totally different type compared to the Secret Service agent whom we had had the honour of encountering. And not only in terms of behaviour, but also appearance. While James was a graceful man, the boy was slender, almost sickly. Our agents were physically fit, but Fawcett's assistant had the typical body of a clerk, already slumped from constant sitting at a desk. He was not ugly, but his face lacked the charisma and piercing confidence of James.

"What do we do? Arrest him and interrogate him?"

"That would only risk hardening his resolve, and he would not reveal the location of the hidden anthrax to us anyway. Besides, after landing he would surely find a way to signal his accomplices where to pick up the shipment."

"So what's your plan?"

"To wait. Let us hang on his heels and see where it will lead us. At the same time we have to shake Gruber, who can complicate things even more."

"Shall we tell Fawcett?"

"I do not consider it necessary," said Holmes, extinguishing his pipe. "The less he knows, the more naturally he will act."

The first day of our investigation in the airship had ultimately proved a success. We were now about halfway through our journey, scheduled to land at Lakehurst early in the morning on May 6.

We were walking to our cabin when a strange thing began to happen around us. Tiny glowing blue lights were flitting wildly all around us, on the railing and on the silver lining of the ship's walls.

"We're on fire!" I cried with terror. "Where are the sparks coming from?"

The detective grabbed my arms to steady me.

"It's not sparks," he said. "It is called St Elmo's fire. It is merely an optical effect created from the discharge of electrically charged particles brought about by the thunderstorm we are now passing through."

"Is it dangerous?"

"Not in the least. Old sailors even considered it a good omen."

The luminous phenomenon slowly subsided, and as we learned in the morning, had been seen by a fair number of the passengers and crew. It was a major topic of conversation at the breakfast table. We were still floating above the ocean, which offered an unchanging view, so the observation deck was not as full of people as on the first day of the flight.

Some passengers were resting in their cabins or hung around the reading room. Fawcett and his assistant prepared for the secretary's mission in the USA throughout the morning. Meanwhile, a specially adapted lightweight piano had been set up in the lounge, as Späh had agreed to stage a performance there.

The passengers were informed of the event via a notice on the bulletin board. There was also a notice that the strong winds and night storms would likely cause a slight delay in our arrival.

Naturally this made the performance all the more welcome. So at four o'clock in the afternoon most of the passengers and crew gathered in the lounge. The stewards had moved the tables to the sides of the room and set up the chairs in rows. When all the chairs had been occupied people stood along the walls. Captains Pruss and Lehmann sat in the first row accompanied by other high-ranking officers as well as Fawcett. His assistant stood behind him, and a few rows back was Gruber.

Späh began the performance, which consisted of a series of humorous songs. I found some funnier than others, but the passengers seemed satisfied and rewarded him with applause.

At around about the third piece, I noticed that Gruber was gone.

I pointed it out to Holmes and together we furtively looked around for the Gestapo officer. That's when I noticed that Fawcett's assistant had left his master and was making his way out of the room.

"Something's happening," the detective whispered. "Maybe this is the chance we've been waiting for. We must follow him!"

Fortunately we were able to follow the Englishman without attracting attention or interfering with the performance. We snuck out, but did not follow the assistant very far, as he had stopped in front of the door to his cabin. One of the stewards was waiting for him there.

The assistant nervously pulled his wallet out of his breast pocket, took out some bills, and shoved them quickly into the steward's hand. With a quick movement the steward counted the money and hid it in his pocket. Then he opened the cabin and the two men entered it.

Just before the door closed we saw them embrace.

My jaw fell to the floor.

"Are you sure that Audrey used *feminine* charms on him?" I gasped.

The detective bit his lower lip. Our theory had fallen apart like a house of cards, and time was inexorably running out. We needed to locate the anthrax in less than twenty-four hours. From the lounge we could hear the sounds of the piano and laughter. It was as though the passengers were mocking our failure.

"No, no, no..." the detective despaired. "My mind is too old and out of shape. Before I would have seen it immediately!"

"But he may still be the prime suspect," I said.

Holmes, however, had immediately devised another theory.

"Watson, there is one other possibility that occurred to me during the night. It makes perfect sense!"

I implored him not to keep me in suspense.

"What if our target is Gruber himself?"

I thought about it. It would mean that Gruber worked both for the Gestapo and the Abwehr. A perfect shadow.

The detective closed his eyes and leaned against the wall. He was not sick, just thinking.

"Let's go," he suddenly cried, and hurried downstairs.

He led me into the room that served as the post office and ordered me to wait outside while he sent a telegram.

"I will no longer stand idly by," he said, explaining that now all we had to do was wait for an answer from the mainland. "It may take several hours, so we might as well watch the end of Späh's performance. Perhaps now that we are almost at the shores of America he will regale us with his satire of the Chancellor. It is said to be hilarious."

I always admired how he managed to free his mind of worry when he knew that at the moment there was nothing to be done. I was never able to accomplish the same trick.

But our downtime did not last long.

Coming towards us along the gangway aft through which I had first followed Späh was Gruber, dragging one of the machinists along behind him. The young man's mouth was gagged. The Gestapo officer was holding him by the neck and shoved him roughly.

He paused momentarily upon seeing us, but had no choice but to continue.

"My God, what is this?" I cried.

"It is none of your concern," he snapped, and dragged the machinist past us up the stairs.

"Mr Gruber, unless you want to cause a commotion, I would suggest that you immediately tell us what you intend to do with that man," Holmes said to him sternly. "The Gestapo's interrogation methods are well-known in England, and this is not your jurisdiction. Stop immediately!"

The German stopped walking, but did not let the machinist go.

"You are defending a murderer who wants to kill us all," he cried. "A saboteur who is determined to blow up this airship and all the people on it!"

The young man flailed and tried to say something through the gag.

"What proof do you have of these allegations?"

The Gestapo was not used to being questioned, let alone by two English pensioners, but he wanted to avoid a scene.

"You are enemies of the Reich and half an hour ago you were the prime suspects," he said. "I do not owe you an explanation!"

Holmes folded his arms.

"You are mistaken," he said calmly. "Our countries have conflicting opinions, but officially we are not at war. We are therefore not enemies of the Reich. And although we are not friends of the Reich, I agree with you that at this moment we are, as they say, in the same boat. If he is indeed a saboteur, we should work together."

Gruber eyed us suspiciously and then again prodded the machinist up the stairs.

"Even if that were the case, you are of no use to me. You are just a couple of civil servants. I have to get this man to tell me where he hid the bomb before it goes off!"

In this he was mistaken.

"If you agree to conduct the interrogation using my methods, I will help you," the detective said, clearing his throat. "Perhaps my name will be familiar. I am Sherlock Holmes and I am a rather proficient criminologist."

XVIII

Hitler's Messenger of Death

The machinist's name was Erich. Gruber had caught him hiding in a section of the ship where he had no business being. When the Gestapo officer spotted him, Erich's shift had already ended and he was sweeping the ship instead of being in his cabin. It was enough to raise Gruber's suspicions.

We went to Gruber's cabin, where the Gestapo officer ordered the machinist to sit on a chair and tied his hands behind his back against the backrest. He kept him gagged for the time being. He locked the door, and stood between it and us as though we too were his prisoners.

"First, explain to me why you are traveling under a false name," he demanded.

If Gruber was the one carrying the anthrax, he would have known about us from Audrey and was just feigning surprise. But we were not sure, so Holmes stepped up his game. I was no longer able to keep track of who knew what about whom.

"I do not wonder at your displeasure," said the detective calmly. "We are traveling incognito in the interests of world peace and to help complete Sir Fawcett's mission. And because we are protected by diplomatic immunity, which your Reich also recognises, you should trust me."

Gruber shrugged.

"I do not have time for these political games," he said. "I will deal with you later. If I do not break this bastard, neither of our missions will matter!"

He tore the gag from the machinist's mouth, grabbed his head and looked him directly in the eyes.

"Where is the bomb?" he shouted. "Where did you hide it?"

"I've done nothing," said Erich. "You do not have the right! I will complain!"

The Gestapo officer pulled him by the straps of his grimy overalls and shook him violently.

"I have all the rights I need, swine!"

He would have slapped him, but the detective stopped him.

"What were you doing back there, young man?" he asked in a considerably milder tone.

But Erich remained defiantly silent. His eyes darted from side to side and he was perspiring. He did not look like an innocent man. He was definitely hiding something.

"Did you want to steal something?" the detective prodded. "Were you trying to get into the cargo hold to search the baggage? You are facing a possible felony charge. Come on, man, give me something that will allow me to help you!"

Meanwhile Gruber pulled out his briefcase and took out Erich's file. He briefly scanned it and then pushed my friend aside. He shoved the documents at the machinist.

"Your lady friend is a well-known Communist activist," he hissed. "Connected to an anti-Nazi organisation. To me this is motive enough for a sabotage attempt... If anything happens to anybody on this ship both you and she will go to the gallows!"

The man was shocked and swallowed hard.

"I don't want the bomb to kill anybody..." he said.

His sudden confession caused a rush of satisfaction to appear on the Gestapo officer's face. He looked at Holmes triumphantly.

"Where is the bomb?" the German shouted. "Tell me where you put it!"

"It will not hurt anybody," Erich insisted and stubbornly refused to divulge any more information.

This time the detective did not stand in Gruber's way as his heavy fist landed on the machinist's face. It tore his skin open and blood flowed out.

It had the desired effect.

"It is timed to the hour when the Hindenburg lands and the passengers have disembarked," Erich spat, glaring at the Gestapo officer. "I am not a killer like you."

"Why are you doing this?" said Holmes.

The machinist raised his chin proudly.

"To show the world that even a giant can burn if it is too proud," he said. "That not all Germans are Adolf Hitler's puppets. I will destroy this cursed propaganda tool once and for all and I do not care what you do to me. There is much more at stake than my life."

"When is the detonator timed? What time does the bomb explode?"

"At the right time."

Erich turned his head and said no more.

Holmes knew that he must let Gruber proceed with his methods. The truth needed to be extracted from the machinist. There was not enough time to search the entire ship.

I glanced at my wristwatch. We would be landing in about twelve hours.

"I will not stay for this," the detective said, looking at Gruber disdainfully and beckoning me to leave.

The Gestapo officer unlocked the door and pushed us into the hallway with a grin. The air on the ship suddenly became stale. I was eager to breathe deeply in a free America.

"Gruber will get what he needs, there is no doubt about it," I said. "He will succeed in preventing the sabotage. But what is our mission? We still do not have the anthrax."

The detective looked at me sadly.

"We must leave Gruber to deal with his current problems, then we will take our turn."

The whole episode had left us feeling drained, so we returned to the others in our company only at dinner, the last on this flight. Holmes had little appetite, but Fawcett did not even notice. He told us is with a wicked smile about the scandal that had broken out after our departure following the performance. Just as my friend had predicted, Späh had performed a parody of Hitler and many of the senior officers had taken offence. Captains Pruss and Lehmann departed in a fury and the first officer subsequently broke up the performance.

We explained that we had left for a stroll in order to rest and to converse on our own.

"And what of the anthrax?" Fawcett said with annoyance. "Tomorrow morning we will land and yet we are emptyhanded."

"Not completely," said Holmes. "I give you my word that we will locate the anthrax."

The old man raised his eyebrows, but did not ask further. He had to trust the detective.

After dinner we stopped in the post office, but the answer to Holmes's telegram had still not arrived.

Then we went to Gruber's cabin. The Gestapo officer barked through the door that the interrogation was still in progress and that we should go away. I did not hear Erich; apparently his interrogator had silenced him.

The detective just shook his head sadly. We could not help the machinist.

So we went to bed, because in the morning an early breakfast awaited us. Outside the weather had again taken a turn for the worse and we were informed that due to the heavy fog we would land a few hours past our scheduled arrival of seven o'clock in the morning.

There was still much left to do.

We found ourselves over the US coast with the first morning light, flying over Boston to New Jersey, where we were expected at the Air Force base in Lakehurst. At breakfast, however, before going to the steering room, Captain Pruss told us that due to the storm clouds we had to adjust course and make a slight detour over Manhattan and across New York. The delays were piling up, making me more and more nervous by the minute.

Holmes too was restless.

"We must at all costs go to Gruber. Erich may have timed the bomb to go off after landing, but now the schedule has changed. The delay may be fatal. We must not let the explosion occur while people are still on board."

I could not disagree with that. I had similar concerns.

While the unsuspecting passengers rejoiced at the detour because it promised a breath-taking view of New York's skyscrapers, we were almost unable to move. We banged on the door of Gruber's cabin until he reluctantly let us in. He gave us a dirty look.

Erich still sat chained to the chair, but it had collapsed. His head had fallen on his chest and his suit was soaked with blood. Gruber's knuckles were red and an open pocket knife lay on the bed. It too was red with blood. It was clear how the night had progressed. The machinist, however, had apparently not talked.

"You're an animal!" I cried, but was met only with an indifferent look.

"I hope you're happy," said Holmes.

I bent down and began to resuscitate the machinist. Moaning and trembling he lifted his head. He had suffered terribly. Instead of a face there was a bloody mess. I reproached myself for letting such a thing happen, for not preventing the interrogation.

"Erich, the ship is late..." said the detective. "We do not know when we will land."

"What time is it?" the prisoner muttered absently.

"It's almost ten in the morning."

"There... is... time," he gasped. With an effort he threw his head back, took a breath and opened his swollen mouth. I noticed that Gruber had smashed most of his teeth.

The man's lax response evidently angered the Gestapo office, and before we knew what was happening, he struck the engineer in the most sensitive area. The man groaned, his eyes turned up in their sockets, and he again fell unconscious. He did not respond to my attempts to revive him, but his wheezing told me he was still alive.

Holmes sent me for my medical bag and I spent the next hour trying to put the tortured prisoner back together. The detective paced back and forth in the cramped quarters like a caged animal, while the disgusted Gestapo officer swung onto the top bunk and stretched out his legs comfortably.

"How can you be so calm?" I wondered. "We might blow up at any moment!"

"If he was speaking the truth, he timed the explosion for late in the evening," said Gruber wearily. "After landing several tours of the Hindenburg are scheduled for visitors. If he wanted to make sure that no one was harmed it cannot be earlier."

The minutes dragged like hours, the hours like days, and the airship still hovered over the coast. Later in the afternoon, when Erich still had not recovered, the Gestapo officer began to falter. All of ours nerves were stretched to breaking point, and we anxiously checked our watches every thirty seconds.

"Should we tell the captain to speed up the landing?" I suggested.

"Landing in a storm is equal to suicide," said Gruber, shaking his head. He too was on tenterhooks. He had not expected Erich to be unconscious for so long, and admitted that he had gone too far in his interrogation. But it did no good. "We are full of volatile hydrogen. One wrong manoeuvre, a single spark of static electricity, and we will go up in flames."

He jumped out of the bed, pushed me aside and shook the machinist roughly.

"Wake up, or you will kill us all!" he shouted.

Erich's eyes slowly opened.

"It's almost night-time! Come on!" Gruber insisted.

The bloody eyes of the beaten boy momentarily brightened.

"Night? Oh God... How long was I unconscious?" he said, groaning.

"Almost all day," I told him. "It's seven o'clock in the evening."

This terrified him, and his reaction terrified us.

"We must move quickly," he said, pulling himself together and trying to get up.

But as he was tied up – Gruber had not let me release him – the chair held him back. He toppled over it and fell on the metal bedframe. We heard the sound of bone cracking.

Erich lay there motionless.

The only one on board who knew the location of the bomb was dead.

Gruber suddenly panicked. He shrieked like a madman, not knowing what to do. The detective recovered first and coolly began to act.

"Run quickly to the wheelhouse," he said, grabbing Gruber by the shoulders. "Do you understand me? We must choose the lesser risk. Tell Captain Pruss to do whatever it takes to land at once and prepare everyone for immediate evacuation!"

Gruber nodded, but I was not sure he really understood what Holmes wanted.

"Watson, you go with him and find Fawcett and his assistant. They will be on the observation deck. We must get them to safety. Tell them what is happening and arrange it."

Then he grabbed the Gestapo man by the arm again.

"Just a moment, Gruber, this is no time for games. Where do you have the anthrax?"

Confused and paralysed with terror, the Gestapo man blinked uncomprehendingly.

"What anthrax? What is it? I don't know what you're talking about."

"He is not lying," said Holmes, looking into his eyes. "Then it is clear..."

We ran out of the cabin and each headed in the opposite direction. The detective for some reason hurried down to the telegraph room, while Gruber and I rushed to the observation deck to find Fawcett.

The passengers were glad that the ship was finally approaching the airport in Lakehurst. I did not want to cause a panic, but fear must have been written on my face. Fortunately the passengers were not paying much attention to what was going on around them, but were gazing out the windows. At the giant hangar that was ready for the Hindenburg a gigantic board had been set up, showing the speed and strength of the wind, according to which the captain conducted the landing. It also showed the time, which was a few minutes after seven o'clock. I breathed a sigh of relief. If everything went well, we would be on the ground in a few minutes. Hopefully before the bomb went off.

I left the Gestapo officer with the surprised Fawcett, and ran back to Holmes.

I collided with him in front of the telegraph room. He was holding in his hand the long-awaited paper. But he did not have time to explain to me what it all meant or what the message contained. Instead he hurried to the restricted area at the rear of the craft.

I kept up with him, but I had to follow behind him, because we were traversing the narrow walkway between the gas tanks. The metal beneath our feet trembled as the vessel descended, leaning according to the movements of the rudder.

We came to the cargo bay where Späh's dog was kept.

Ulla and Fawcett's terrier were upset because they could feel the Hindenburg's wild manoeuvres. When they saw us, they began to bark loudly and banged their heads against the bars of their cages. Holmes stopped in front of the terrier's cage, opened the door and took the dog in his arms. I thought that he wanted to save it before the explosion.

Instead, he removed the collar with its clanking pendants and placed the dog on the ground.

He tore off one of the pendants and examined it closely. On it he found a hinge, which he opened. He tilted it over and a small vial dropped into his palm. The anthrax with which Adolf Hitler wanted to sow chaos in the United States had finally been found!

"I assume that all ten pendants on the collar contain similar vials," he said triumphantly.

"Truly an intervention at the eleventh hour, as the saying goes," said a voice behind us.

We turned around. On the walkway behind us hobbled Fawcett, dressed in an overcoat. I was shocked to see him out of his wheelchair. He shuffled slowly, leaning on a stick. His legs apparently were not as bad as it seemed.

"I must applaud you," he added. "I suppose you have not yet succumbed entirely to senility."

The terrier ran in his direction but completely ignored his master. It just ran past him and scurried toward the passenger part of the airship.

Once again I had missed something crucial.

Fawcett pulled a Luger pistol from his coat and pointed it at us.

XIX

Death above New Jersey

Fawcett extended his hand and demanded the return of the collar with its deadly contents. Holmes hesitated. The Hindenburg was already landing and he was playing for time. Not with the bomb, but with our counterpart.

"If you shoot now, you will ignite the gas in the balloons and kill yourself together with everyone on board," Holmes said. "It is probably not necessary."

Fawcett's still bright blue eyes, which once upon a time had attracted my attention, expressed a sea of indifference. Agent Methuselah, as Leonard had called him, saw human life as something expendable.

"You of all people should know that for men of our age the threat of death loses its menace. On the contrary, it becomes a reward for a job well done."

He said it so carelessly that I did not believe he really intended to commit suicide. He leaned on the railing, put down his stick, reached into his pocket and pulled out a shiny metal object that he screwed onto the barrel of his pistol.

The vessel swung sharply and the walkway inclined as the ship's prow descended more quickly than the stern.

"The scientists of the Abwehr have assured me that I can shoot this on board without risking fire," said Fawcett. "It extinguishes all sparks."

"Do you not understand that delivering anthrax into the hands of the local fascists could inflict incalculable damage on our allies?" said Holmes.

"Your allies, not mine," said Fawcett.

"What on earth has led you to change sides in old age?" I said uncomprehendingly. I could not understand what would lead a British diplomat into the arms of the Nazis and convince him to help them attack the United States. The political consequences could be terrible.

The detective replied for him.

"The honourable Frederick Fawcett has not changed sides, my dear Watson," he said. "On the contrary, he remains faithful to what he has been serving for fifty years, if I am not mistaken."

"If I did not need both hands I would applaud," said the treacherous secretary. "What took you so long to figure it out?"

"My unwillingness to believe what seemed so far-fetched," my friend sighed. "Indeed, I recently told the doctor that all these years of retirement have numbed my senses and that I have stopped following my own rules."

"Does this mean that Fawcett has been a German spy for over half a century?" I said with disbelief.

"Yes," Holmes shrugged. "It finally makes sense to me how Tanuja got access to Queen Victoria. And I daresay that even his clumsiness, which allowed her to escape from the palace, had me fooled. It is also why nobody ever succeeded in finding her. Somebody sabotaged the investigation. Our dear Fawcett was already serving Kaiser Wilhelm and now he has simply exchanged one militant fanatic for another."

"You well know that Victoria was hardly an ambassador for peace," Fawcett countered.

The detective refused to be drawn into an argument.

"Were I not so short-sighted and burdened by emotion and judged only by the facts, I would have already revealed your true nature in Frankfurt," he continued, as though oblivious to the pistol pointed at him or the jerky movements of the descending airship.

"Really?" said Fawcett. "What did I do wrong?"

"Our group passed through customs control with remarkable ease, even though we were suspicious. His supervisor had to command him to let us go. Your dog was also the only thing that didn't go through the inspection at all. And you were also one of only a handful of people who could have told Audrey about our mission. But although I toyed with the idea in my head, I refused to believe it, and instead sought motives elsewhere. And when finally I received a telegram telling me that you had never owned a dog, the truth could no longer be avoided."

"But… but why?" I said, still looking for an answer to the same question.

The sullen Fawcett apparently decided that he at least owed us this absolution.

"Have you ever studied genealogy, Doctor? I have. The fascinating world of pedigrees and family ties. Had you had the chance to study my family line far enough you would have discovered my affiliation to a noble family whose right to the throne was robbed. History only had to take a small step in a different direction and you would be speaking to me now as your king!"

"A fine king," I spat.

"Even so my family had enough influence to set me on the path of an illustrious political career. Why do you think that England's power has weakened so much over the past decade? I did everything I could to reveal the weakness and incompetence of the House of Windsor!"

The hands of the man who would be king were shaking as he pointed the gun at us.

"All right, they denied you the throne. But why do you want to plunge the world into war?"

"Because in the new order after the German victory the Führer has assured me a fitting position! My family and I shall return to our rightful place. Even though you have taken away my granddaughter's future as the princess…"

"Your granddaughter?"

Holmes, unlike me, received this latest information with stoic calm.

"Indeed you have thoroughly instilled your beliefs in Audrey," he said coldly. "A pity that it did not occur to me to investigate the connection earlier."

Fawcett glanced at his watch. It was almost half past seven.

"Time is running out," said the traitor, cocking his pistol.

"How do you plan to explain our death?"

"As the first victims of an inevitable war," he said. "According to what the doctor said, somewhere in this ship a bomb set by an ideological madman is slowly ticking. I suppose that it will soon explode. The investigation will no doubt prove that the sabotage threat was real and that you were simply in the wrong place at the wrong time."

"Unlike you the boy did not want to hurt anyone," said the detective.

"Give me the collar!" Fawcett shouted, losing patience. "Come on!"

From what Erich had said the explosion could occur at any second. I wondered if I would rather die at the hands of a traitor or burn with the whole airship. I must admit that I favoured the second option, even though it meant that everyone on board would die. At least the anthrax would burn too, which would prevent the loss of hundreds or even thousands of lives. The good of the many outweighed the good of the few.

Holmes stood clutching the collar in one hand and the vial containing the poison in the other. I knew that he would never give it up. Perhaps he intended to crush the vial and hurl its contents at Fawcett.

But he did not have time to do anything.

Neither did Fawcett.

Nor I.

We were suddenly surrounded by a bright yellow light. Then my brain registered the rumbling sound of explosions. The bomb had to be somewhere at the rear, close to us. What I describe took only a few seconds, perhaps half a minute at most, but to me it seemed like a lifetime flashing before my eyes.

Immediately I knew what had happened. Fawcett lost his balance and dropped the gun. It clanged on the walkway and fell down somewhere. Then suddenly the prow lifted and Holmes and I could barely stay on our feet.

There were flames. Deep yellow, glowing and ubiquitous. Fawcett didn't have a chance. He did not even have time to scream for help as he fell forward toward us.

It seemed like the air was on fire. In the blaze the detective lost the collar and the vial with the anthrax, but it did not matter. The raging inferno engulfed it and forever destroyed it.

I did not know if the ghostly wail that tore through our ears was coming from Fawcett as he died or from someone else or from the bowels of the ship that the fire was devouring with lightning speed. Ulla, Späh's puppy, mercifully died immediately. In the hot, melting cage she had nowhere to escape.

The metal braces buckled like matchsticks, more explosions echoed, and the ship fell like a stone. The gas tanks cracked, feeding the fire more fuel. From inside the airship we saw the outer shell disappear and suddenly the sky above our heads.

I pulled Holmes behind me, instinctively away from the fire, but it was faster than me. Then from somewhere came a gust of wind, blowing the flames away from us.

We scrambled off the walkway, raised across the ladder to the lower deck. We were saved from the worst flames by the wardroom, into which we ran for cover.

Above it were the ship's water tanks, which had just burst. In an instant the burning heat that had surrounded us gave way to a rush of cooling water that soaked us to the skin. The deck trembled in the final death throes of the proud airship.

We ran as fast as we could. I do not know how we got into one of the rooms on the starboard side, but we did. Through the windows, which had been smashed, I could see the ground rapidly approaching. We must have fallen from a height of some six or seven hundred feet.

Below us terrified members of the ground crew were fleeing from the site of the impact. They stared up at us with horrified expressions, crossing themselves and crying. In the distance I could see the flashes of cameras.

Before the window hung a rain-drenched rope used to pull the ship to the landing pad. Flaming debris was falling all around us as the Hindenburg collapsed and burned.

People were jumping from the other windows to escape the flames. I recognised the terrified faces of our fellow passengers and crew members.

"Watson, this is our only chance!" Holmes shouted.

He shoved into me and almost threw me onto the rope, which was dangling just in front of me. He saved my life. I grabbed the rope and swung down, landing on the lawn and stumbling away from the falling behemoth. My old and decrepit body was shaking, my bones and muscles groaned, but I could not stop. I was still not out of danger. It could crush me beneath it like a flea.

The detective was behind me, but I did not have time to watch him.

I felt behind me the gigantic, majestic disaster. I ran as fast as I could, until exhaustion got the better of me and I fell into someone's arms.

Erich the machinist had defeated Goliath. But at a terrible price.

XX

Reckoning

When I later saw newsreel footage of the disaster and the emotional commentary of the reporter, I did not understand how I could have survived. Thirty-six others did not have the same good fortune on May 6, 1937. Thirteen passengers, twenty-two crew members and one man from the ground crew died. Most of them burned to death inside the ship, others died while jumping from the windows, and others were hit by falling debris or suffocated.

Captain Pruss survived, although he lay for a long time in hospital and his face remains forever scarred by ugly burns. After returning to Germany, he became the head of the Frankfurt airport.

The second captain whom we met during the trip, Ernst Lehmann, died a day after the disaster. He had managed to escape the ship like I had, but the injuries he suffered were too severe. The doctors believed they could save him, and the officer even gave testimony from his hospital bed, but then he took a turn for the worse.

Joseph Späh survived thanks to his acrobatic training. He too had jumped out of the window, suffering only a twisted ankle.

Fawcett's assistant died just like his master. His body was found in the ruins, charred beyond recognition. Whether he had died in the accident or Fawcett had killed him before going to the cargo bay was never determined. The small terrier, which the secretary had used to smuggle the anthrax, had miraculously escaped the ship. For some reason she came to me at the airport and would not leave me. I decided to adopt her right then and there, and named her Buffy.

The fate of the Gestapo man Gruber remains unclear. His body was not found after the accident, but nobody had seen him among the survivors at the airport either.

As for me, I was treated at Lakehurst by Dr Raymond Taylor. I was among the fortunate few with only minor injuries. I left the airport on foot and stayed in a nearby hotel.

Holmes had had a rougher time of it. For the first few nights I was worried that he would not survive. But he was a fighter, and soon his condition began to improve.

Often in those days as he was recovering and I began to jot down notes about this adventure, he feverishly repeated that if he died, he wanted to be buried in nearby Trenton. That was the final resting place of his old flame, Irene Adler. He took a morbid pleasure in the symbolism of it.

But in the end, he lived.

The newspapers speculated for a long time about the cause of the tragedy. There were several theories. Some claimed that the landing had been too abrupt, causing the vessel to buckle under the strain. Others even suggested that Hitler himself had ordered the ship's destruction. The actual explanation, which only a few people knew, was never confirmed.

The official FBI investigation concluded that the disaster may have been caused by a spark of static electricity. The German, British and American governments were all interested in this result. It was the only chance to keep the world from falling into the abyss, at least for a little while longer. The Germans did not claim Sir Fawcett and instead tried to blame the British Secret Service, accusing it of conspiring with the United States. It was a diplomatic standoff that ended when all records about the existence of the traitor and his rotten family were lost in the dustbin of history.

Evidence of the sabotage was destroyed. Although the chairman of the Zeppelin Company, Hugo Eckener, and other officers tried to save the reputation of airships and find evidence of sabotage, in the end most were convinced to cooperate. The golden age of airships had come to an end.

I must not forget our friends from Fulworth.

Obviously we did not attend Richard's funeral, for it took place during our investigation. We were glad to have this excuse, because we did not want to attend it. Our protégé had fallen victim to his passions and desires, and we could not forgive what he had done. But we kept it to ourselves. There was no reason to tell his parents the truth. In the end we even gave them Richard's money.

Major Steiner got home safely, recovered and remained with his wife in our service. We never learned whether James survived the fall, but I am sure that his name, synonymous with the very best of the British Secret Service, will live on.

Fildes's research into the military applications of the microbe *Bacillus anthraxis* at Porton Down continued for some time. But in the end it was not used and the project was cancelled. After all, something with a potentially much greater killing power was discovered, but this time in the field of physics. They too, however, focused on the tiniest of particles... The atom.

And what of Sherlock Holmes after his recovery?

In the foreword to this story I apologised for lying to you in the past. So please, do not ask me…

I would have to reoffend.

Also From Petr Macek

Europe 1911. The Great Powers vie for influence and are divided by political quarrels. War is in the air. For retired detective Sherlock Holmes, who has just suffered a coronary, these distant matters are of little concern. But politics are about to turn his quiet country life upside down. Mycroft, the detective's politician brother, has asked Holmes to investigate the murder of a powerful industrialist and the mysterious kidnapping of the King's nephew. Could these two cases be connected? Thus the legendary detective and his old friend Watson set out on an all-new adventure, one that will take them from the canals of Venice to an ancient castle in the Scottish plains. It's an adventure they could hardly have expected as they near the ripe old age of sixty. Will Holmes lose a lifelong friend? And which villain from Holmes's past might want to start a world war...?

Also from Petr Macek

Reichenbach was not his deepest fall.... Autumn 1903 has not been kind to Sherlock Holmes. Irene Adler, his platonic love, is dead, and the detective has again fallen into the clutches of cocaine. Dr Watson hopes that the distraction of a marriage fraud case can help pull his friend out of his depression. But it soon becomes clear that behind the apparently banal crime lurks something much more sinister, something that will take Holmes and Watson to faraway Bohemia, where they must face an unimaginably terrible enemy. A corpse has been discovered on the grave of Rabbi Loew and Prague's Jews are whispering about the Golem...

Also from MX Publishing

MX Publishing is the world's largest specialist Sherlock Holmes publisher, with over a hundred titles and fifty authors creating the latest in Sherlock Holmes fiction and non-fiction.

From traditional short stories and novels to travel guides and quiz books, MX Publishing cater for all Holmes fans.

The collection includes leading titles such as *Benedict Cumberbatch In Transition* and *The Norwood Author* which won the 2011 Howlett Award (Sherlock Holmes Book of the Year).

MX Publishing also has one of the largest communities of Holmes fans on Facebook with regular contributions from dozens of authors.

www.mxpublishing.com

Also from MX Publishing

The Missing Authors Series

Sherlock Holmes and The Adventure of The Grinning Cat
Sherlock Holmes and The Nautilus Adventure
Sherlock Holmes and The Round Table Adventure

"Joseph Svec, III is brilliant in entwining two endearing and enduring classics of literature, blending the factual with the fantastical; the playful with the pensive; and the mischievous with the mysterious. We shall, all of us young and old, benefit with a cup of tea, a tranquil afternoon, and a copy of Sherlock Holmes, The Adventure of the Grinning Cat."
Amador County Holmes Hounds Sherlockian Society

www.mxpublishing.com

Also from MX Publishing

The Detective and The Woman Series

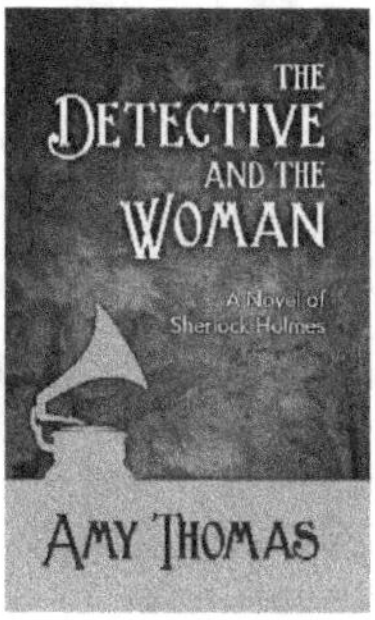

The Detective and The Woman
The Detective, The Woman and The Winking Tree
The Detective, The Woman and The Silent Hive

"The book is entertaining, puzzling and a lot of fun. I believe the author has hit on the only type of long-term relationship possible for Sherlock Holmes and Irene Adler. The details of the narrative only add force to the romantic defects we expect in both of them and their growth and development are truly marvelous to watch. This is not a love story. Instead, it is a coming-of-age tale starring two of our favorite characters."
Philip K Jones

Also from MX Publishing

The American Literati Series

The Final Page of Baker Street
The Baron of Brede Place
Seventeen Minutes To Baker Street

"The really amazing thing about this book is the author's ability to call up the 'essence' of both the Baker Street 'digs' of Holmes and Watson as well as that of the 'mean streets' of Marlowe's Los Angeles. Although none of the action takes place in either place, Holmes and Watson share a sense of camaraderie and self-confidence in facing threats and problems that also pervades many of the later tales in the Canon. Following their conversations and banter is a return to Edwardian England and its certainties and hope for the future. This is definitely the world before The Great War."
Philip K Jones

www.mxpublishing.com